HATE AT FIRST SIGHT

From the moment Deborah met the Duke of Gretton, he filled her with rage. Let others call him devilishly handsome, charming, wealthy, powerful, and the most eligible lord in the realm. Let the brilliant and ravishing actress Kate Hatherley revel in her role as his latest mistress.

As for Deborah, she thought him insufferably rude, arrogant, selfish, and supremely self-centered—quite the most repulsive so-called gentleman she had ever encountered.

Until now, at this ball . . . as he whirled her in a dizzying dance . . . as he apologized to her in the most elegant way for his boorish behavior . . . as he exquisitely kissed her hand before driving off in his carriage.

Deborah remained where she was. She could still feel the touch of his lips upon her hand, and it was a sensation which made her feel unaccountably vulnerable. It had been so much easier to despise him, for there was safety in hostility. . . .

LADY SABRINA'S SECRET

by

Sandra Heath

A SIGNET BOOK

SIGNET
Published by the Penguin Group
Penguin Books USA Inc., 375 Hudson Street,
New York, New York 10014, U.S.A.
Penguin Books Ltd, 27 Wrights Lane,
London W8 5TZ, England
Penguin Books Australia Ltd, Ringwood,
Victoria, Australia
Penguin Books Canada Ltd, 10 Alcorn Avenue,
Toronto, Ontario, Canada M4V 3B2
Penguin Books (N.Z.) Ltd, 182–190 Wairau Road,
Auckland 10, New Zealand

Penguin Books Ltd, Registered Offices:
Harmondsworth, Middlesex, England

First published by Signet, an imprint of New American Library,
a division of Penguin Books USA Inc.

First Printing, May, 1993
10 9 8 7 6 5 4 3 2

Chapter 1

A fierce March wind roared in from the open sea, and huge waves crashed against the rocky Dorset shore as the storm reached its height. Both sea and sky were leaden in color, so that the horizon was blurred and indistinct, and far out on the water a naval brig fled before the gale, her sails straining so much that it seemed they must soon rip from the masts. Spindrift flew through the salt-laden air, and the screams of gulls resounded all around as the lone horsewoman rode to the top of the windswept cliffs and then reined in to look down into the narrow cove below.

Deborah Marchant was twenty-seven years old and very striking, with a creamy complexion, large gray eyes, and heavy black curls that were piled up beneath her brown beaver hat. She wore a russet riding habit, and the white gauze scarf tied around the crown of her hat whipped and flapped as if it wanted to fly away inland over the mellow Dorset countryside. The horse was uneasy, but she controlled it with almost absent-minded ease, her attention upon the seething white-flecked waves thundering against the rocks at the foot of the cliffs.

There were tears in her eyes as she watched the fury of the storm, for it was here, on a day like this three years ago, that her husband's frigate had been driven on to the rocks, and he and all his crew had perished. The loss of HMS *Thetis* had shocked the whole of England, for the storm had sprung up within minutes and had gone again just as quickly, leaving devastation in its wake. There was no trace now of the doomed frigate, and Captain Jonathan Marchant and many of his crew lay buried in his nearby home village of St. Mary Magna, which nestled so safely in a fold of the hills, protected from the gales that sometimes swept in so willfully from the ocean.

As Deborah continued to look down into the cove, it seemed that the din of the storm became suddenly muffled, and she could hear Jonathan's parting words to her. *I will not be away for more than four months, my darling, and if I can be with you for our anniversary, then I swear I will. I love you, Deborah.*

The *Thetis* had set sail from Portsmouth, beating eastward into the storm, and cruel fate had decreed not only that he and his crew should perish before they had a chance to engage the French, but that they should do so right here, within a mile of his home. She had slept through the tragedy, and the first she knew of what had happened had been when the vicar of St. Mary's had come to break the news as gently as he could.

The three years had passed now, but the grief was sometimes as fresh as if it had only been three months ago. When the wind blew like this, the pain was most keen, piercing her with grief and guilt, for she could not forgive herself that while Jonathan had been meeting his death, she had slept safe and unknowing in their bed. Intuition should have aroused her; she should have sensed that he was in mortal danger. But nothing had disturbed her dreams, nothing at all.

Tears were wet on her cheeks as she gathered the reins and turned her horse away from the clifftops. She rode wildly, trying to use the exhilaration of the gallop to stem the flow of the tears. The land sloped gradually away from the cliffs, and soon the noise of the sea began to dwindle away behind her. Ahead of her the gentle Dorset countryside rolled away inland, as wooded and beautiful as the shore was savage and bleak, and in a valley that followed the course of the little River Chaldon rose the tower of St. Mary's church.

The daffodils were out in the gardens of St. Mary Magna, and there was blossom on the trees. The rambling thatched cottages had stood so long beside the river that they seemed to have grown out of the earth without the help of human hands. Smoke was whisked away from the chimneys, but the wind did not reach right down to the winding road that led toward the church and the manor house, her home from the moment she'd married Jonathan some six years before.

She reined in briefly by the lych-gate of the churchyard, her gaze drawn unwillingly toward the Marchant family chapel, which had been built on to the church in the fifteenth century when the Marchants had become lords of St. Mary Magna. Jonathan lay there now with his forebears, and she was alone with her memories. They had been so much in love, and so very, very happy together that they had never dreamed they would have so little time. All their hopes had ended the day the *Thetis* foundered on the rocks, and with Jonathan's death the Marchant line had become extinct, for she had never given him a child. They had planned to have such a large family, to fill the house with voices and laughter. . . .

More tears stung her eyes, and she urged her horse on again, past the churchyard wall and in through the wrought iron gates of the manor house. The gravel drive was not long and passed through grounds that were bright with daffodils and crocuses. It finished in a circular area that was wide enough for a carriage-and-six to turn with ease, and the arched, iron-studded doorway was approached up a flight of four steps. The house itself dated from the beginning of the fifteenth century and was dominated by a huge oriel window on the first floor. This window faced down the village street and now simply enjoyed a fine view of the river and cottages, but once it had given warning of approaching enemies. There were no longer any enemies; nor were there any Marchants to be on their guard.

Her horse kicked up the gravel as she drew it to a standstill by the door, and a groom hurried from the stables at the rear of the house to take the reins. Her return would have been anticipated from the moment she'd begun the descent from the clifftops, for she would have been clearly visible from the stable yard. The groom gave her a curious glance as he saw her tears, and he paused to gaze after her as she hastened into the house without giving him the customary word of thanks. But then he glanced up at the racing clouds overhead and remembered.

As the main door swung to behind her, Deborah's steps faltered, and she halted for a moment in the great hall to try to regain her composure. She'd been foolish to ride up to the cliffs on a day like this, for the memories were bound to be particularly painful. She blinked the tears away fiercely. She wouldn't give in, she wouldn't! She must take a grip on herself, for it was long since time that she took up her life again instead of hiding away in seclusion like this. Her friends despaired of her, and her brother Richard was thoroughly vexed. Richard was a carefree bachelor who enjoyed society life to the full, and even though he had sympathized greatly with her when Jonathan had first died, the commencement of a third year without her showing any inclination to rejoin the *beau monde* had made him cross with her, a fact he'd made very plain indeed on the last of his infrequent visits.

Taking a steadying breath, she put her riding crop down on a table and began to tease off her gloves. The hall was old and very comfortable, with a stone floor that was worn with age, magnificent oak paneling on the walls, and furniture of such antiquity that at least one chair was older than the house itself. There were crimson velvet curtains on either side of the doors and windows, and bowls of spring flowers on the tables, so that everything was cheerful, but still her sadness intruded today.

"Madam?" The butler's voice made her start.

"Yes, Briggs? What is it?" She turned as he emerged from the shadows beyond the foot of the staircase at the far end of the hall. He should have retired by now but was most unwilling to do so, and she did not like to offend him by suggesting that it might be time he enjoyed the cottage that had been set aside for him. He had once been tall and ramrod straight but now was bent and frail, with a powdered wig to conceal his completely bald head. He wore a blue coat and dark gray breeches, and his brown eyes were watery as he picked up a silver tray from one of the tables. There was a brown paper package on the tray, and he held it out to her.

"This has arrived for you by special messenger, madam. It is from Mr. Wexford and appears to be rather urgent."

From Richard? Deborah was rather taken aback, for it was unheard of to receive a communication of any kind from her brother. His visits were always unannounced, and in between there were months of absolute silence. Puzzled, she took the package. It was very tightly tied with string, and a great deal of sealing wax had been used to make certain it could not be easily opened. What on earth could it be?

Briggs bowed to her. "Madam, I have taken the liberty of having some tea served in the winter parlor."

"Mm? Oh, yes. Thank you, Briggs, that was most thoughtful." Deborah looked up from studying the package and smiled at him.

"Madam." Bowing once more, he withdrew.

Deciding not to open the package until she was comfortably seated with a dish of tea, she gathered her rather cumbersome russet skirts and hastened to the grand staircase to go up to the winter parlor on the floor above.

A moment or so later she was warmly ensconced in a high-backed chair by the fireplace, with the March daylight filtering into the room behind her from the huge oriel window. In the distance were the windswept cliffs, and closer lay the matchless view along the village street, but her attention was solely upon the package.

Splinters of sealing wax fell onto her lap as she undid the string, and as she unfolded the paper she saw that the package contained a small box and a letter. In the box there was a gentleman's gold pocket watch of such exquisite workmanship that the Prince Regent himself would have been proud to own it. Diamonds and pearls were studded around the case, and when she opened it she saw an inscription on the inside. *To my beloved Richard, my love always, Sabrina. The tenth of March, 1811.*

The tenth of March, exactly one week ago, had been Richard's twenty-ninth birthday, and so the timepiece was evidently a birthday gift from a sweetheart, Sabrina. But why on earth had he sent it here to St. Mary Magna? No doubt all would be revealed in the letter.

Resting the letter on her lap to read, she picked up her dish of tea and sipped it. The address at the top of the letter was Royal Crescent, Bath, which meant that he was staying with their old friends, Henry and Jenny Masterson, who resided there with Jenny's widowed aunt, the ebullient and singular Mrs. McNeil. The Mastersons came from the same part of Herefordshire as the Wexfords, and their friendship with Richard and Deborah went back to childhood. Deborah was a little surprised to realize her brother was in Bath, for she had believed him to be in his lodgings in London's Bond Street.

She began to read the letter, and almost immediately her heart sank with dismay and disbelief, for what she read was very troubling indeed.

My dearest Deborah,
No matter what you might read of me in the news-papers in the coming days, I am innocent of all wrong-doing, but fate has left me no choice except to go into hiding. My arrest is imminent, and I must flee if I am to save myself from the conspiracy of my one-time

friend, Sir James Uppingham, and his unlikely partner in crime, Lady Ann Appleby.

Deborah stared at the letter. Wrongdoing? Arrest? Conspiracy? Her hand trembled, and she put her dish of tea down upon the table before continuing to read.

The pocket watch I enclose with this letter is more precious to me than you can ever know, for it was given to me by the woman I will always love with all my heart, and who would still love me were it not for this conspiracy to ruin my good name and honor. If all had gone as we planned, she and I would have eloped by now, but instead she believes only ill of me, and has decided to continue with a match arranged this long time by her family. How can I blame her when she has been led to believe that not only am I a thief, but also that I have been deceiving her with Lady Ann?

Deborah, I am not a thief, no matter what Uppingham may pretend to have seen, and I would never play Sabrina false with anyone, I love her too completely for that.

Please keep the watch safe for me at St. Mary Magna, tell no one of its existence, and above all do not mention Sabrina's name to anyone. I wish to protect her now, and can only do that by staying out of her life. She is not strong, and is terrified of scandal.

Henry and Jenny know nothing of Sabrina, nor does Mrs. McNeil, for I have kept my own counsel, as well I should as I have been conducting a secret affair which would shock society were it ever to come to light.

Forgive me for embroiling you, but I could not think of anywhere else to send the pocket watch and be certain of its safekeeping. No one must ever know that

*Sabrina gave me a gift with such an inscription at the
very time when her family was proceeding with plans
for her betrothal.*

*I do not know where I will go now, but I will write
to you again when I can. Please do not think ill of me
for fleeing and thus exposing the family name to
odium.*

Believe in me, I beg of you.

Your loving brother,
Richard.

Shaken, Deborah slowly put the letter aside and then
rose to her feet. Was it really possible that such things
had happened to her brother? She went to the oriel
window and stared down the village street. What had
really gone on in Bath? Why had Richard been falsely
accused by this Sir James Uppingham and by Lady
Ann Appleby? What reason could they have for so
wickedly conspiring against him? And who was the
mysterious Sabrina, whose name was to be protected
at all costs? She had to be a lady of some wealth to be
able to afford a timepiece as valuable as the one she
had had so lovingly inscribed.

Deborah exhaled slowly. She felt so helpless, and
so very, very angry, for there was nothing she could
do to help, and she didn't even know where Richard
was.

She thought about the letter. Richard had mentioned
that she might read about it all in the newspapers.
Perhaps she would learn more when she did. Then,
depending upon what she discovered, she would decide what to do. Richard needed her, and she would
not fail him, nor would she stand idly by and allow
him to be the victim of others' villainy. If she felt that

there was anything to gain by going to Bath to make inquiries of her own, then that was what she would do. Her three years of self-imposed seclusion would be brought to an end in the cause of clearing her brother's name and bringing the real culprits to justice.

Chapter 2

It was still stormy and overcast the next morning when Deborah awoke after a restless, virtually sleepless night. She'd tossed and turned anxiously because of Richard and had been lying staring at the tester over her bed for a long time when at last her maid came with the morning tea.

Amy Jenkinson had been with her ever since she'd married Jonathan and come to St. Mary Magna, indeed the maid had been born in the village, and her family had served the Marchants for generations. She was a neat, fair-haired young woman with pale blue eyes and freckles, and she wore a fresh green-and-white gingham dress, a white apron, and a starched mobcap. She placed the tea beside her mistress's bed, and then went to draw back the curtains.

The pale March daylight brightened the room, but coldly so, and with a shiver the maid went to do what she could to poke the embers of the fire into more life. As Amy knelt before the hearth, Deborah sat up in the bed, reaching over the coverlet for her warm shawl and putting it around her shoulders. Her coal black curls tumbled over her shoulders, and her gray eyes were tired as she picked up the dish of tea.

The room was the one she and Jonathan had shared

and was the largest bedroom in the house. It faced over the walled garden and bowling green at the rear of the house and boasted no fewer than three embrasured windows set deep into the thick stone outer wall. Inside it was paneled, and there were tapestries depicting scenes from medieval romances. There were rugs on the polished wooden floor and a yellow brocade armchair by the fire. The four-poster bed was hung with white silk, and through the archway in the wall there was a dressing room where the same white silk had been draped over the dressing table. At the windows the curtains were made of yellow velvet, forming a bright frame for the gray March day outside.

At last Amy coaxed some flames from the fire, and quickly she selected a suitable log from the rack beside the hearth, pressing it firmly onto the fire before getting to her feet again and coming to the foot of the bed.

"What shall you wear today, madam?"

"Oh, the pink-and-white dimity, I think," Deborah replied.

"Yes, madam." Amy hesitated, looking at her in some concern. "Is everything all right, madam?" she asked, taking in Deborah's pale face and tired eyes.

"I didn't sleep very well, that's all," Deborah answered. She hadn't said anything about Richard, nor did she intend to until she knew more.

"Madam, I . . ." Amy couldn't say whatever was on her mind and lowered her eyes self-consciously.

"Yes, Amy? What is it?"

"I know it isn't my place, madam, but I was just going to beg you not to go riding up on the cliffs to remember things today. It's very windy again, and it does you no good to go up there when it's like this."

The maid's face was red, and she kept her gaze lowered. "Begging your pardon for having spoken out of turn, madam," she added.

Deborah managed a smile. "Thank you for your concern, Amy, and you may rest assured that I will not go up on the cliffs again."

"Yes, madam."

As the maid turned to go through into the dressing room to select the pink-and-white dimity gown from the wardrobe, Deborah suddenly remembered what Richard's letter had warned her to expect. "Amy, has the newspaper arrived yet?"

"Yes, madam. It awaits you in the breakfast room as usual."

"I wish to see it now, if you please."

"Now? Yes, madam." Amy was obviously a little surprised by such an order, for it was always her mistress's custom to read the newspaper at the breakfast table, never in the bedroom.

As the maid hurried out once more, Deborah finished her tea and then replaced the cup and saucer on the little cabinet by the bed. Then she hesitated a moment before bending down to pull open the drawer in the cabinet and take out the package and letter that had arrived the day before. For a long moment she studied the timepiece again, and then ran her fingertips over the inscription. Whoever the mysterious Sabrina was, Richard was deeply in love with her still, even though she had chosen to spurn him and believe ill of him.

With a heavy sigh she replaced the things in the drawer, and then took out something else she always kept there. It was an oval gold locket on a chain, and it contained a likeness of Jonathan and a lock of his hair arranged like a feather. The portrait was an excellent one, bringing him to life again in a way which sometimes caused her pain. It was a head-and-shoulders representation of him in his naval uniform, set against a blue sky with white clouds. His green eyes smiled warmly at her, and the artist had captured his luxuriant chestnut hair so well that it was almost as if the sea breeze were ruffling through it.

She heard Amy returning and replaced the locket in the drawer. The maid brought the morning mail as well as the newspaper, and when she had given both to her mistress she went through into the dressing room. Deborah sat by the fire, and began to glance through the newspaper first. She did not have long to search before Richard's name seemed to leap out at her.

It is reported that Mr. Richard Wexford of Wexford Park, Herefordshire, and of Bond Street, London, is being sought on a charge of theft, having purloined a diamond necklace from the home of Lady Ann Appleby, into whose good offices he had apparently inserted himself with the sole view of relieving her of her jewels. The necklace was removed from the bedroom of Lady Ann's house in Great Pulteney Street, Bath, and the identity of the thief might never have been known had it not been that Mr. Wexford unwisely secreted the necklace in his carriage, where his efforts to keep it concealed were witnessed by his friend, Sir James Uppingham. Sir James subsequently retrieved Lady Ann's property. Mr. Wexford has since fled the city, and is still being hunted. It is to be hoped that he will shortly be apprehended and brought to account.

Deborah refolded the newspaper, and then leaned her head back against the chair. Well, at least she now knew exactly what her brother was accused of doing, and she had Richard's word that Sir James Uppingham and Lady Ann Appleby were co-conspirators against him. And very clever conspirators they were, too, for with evidence such as theirs, it was hardly surprising that the timid-hearted Sabrina believed herself betrayed and let down by the man with whom she'd planned to elope.

Closing her eyes for a moment, Deborah then turned her attention briefly to the mail. Almost immediately she saw a letter in the familiar hand of her old friend, Jenny Masterson, at whose residence Richard had been staying when the scandal began. Breaking the seal, she quickly began to read.

> *Royal Crescent, Bath.*
> *March 15th, 1811.*

Dearest Deborah,

I have no doubt that by now you will have heard the shocking things which are being said of poor Richard, who has not helped his cause at all by fleeing. Needless to say, we in this household are stout in his defense and have been censured on account of it. Sir James Uppingham and Lady Ann Appleby pretend not to know each other, but must do. They are clever.

Knowing you as well as I do after all this time, I can imagine that your furious indignation on his behalf will prise you from your Dorset lair. Please do not hesitate to come to us, for you are more than welcome, and besides, with the Bath season at its height, accommodation is at a premium.

Having issued this invitation, I must now confess that it may be that Henry and I will be called away to Herefordshire. *His father is ill at the moment, and his mother has warned us to expect to be sent for. I trust not, but she is not a lady to issue such warnings without reason. However, the house will not be empty, for Aunt McNeil will be here, and as you would expect of her, there is no one in Bath who is more fierce in Richard's support. She and Lady Ann were friends until all this, but that friendship is no more. By the way, in case you are not acquainted with Lady Ann, she is the very prim spinster daughter of the Earl of Harandon, and at fifteen years Richard's senior, is not at all his type. We both know that his preference is for dependent young things of an adoring nature, but I fear that Lady Ann, although still reckoned very beautiful, is none of those things. It is therefore a nonsense to credit him with having an affair with her, even in order to steal her wretched necklace.*

Be strong, my dear friend, and please come to us if you wish. I must warn you, though, that although we in this house are Richard's friends, the rest of Bath society is convinced of his guilt.

> *Your loyal and affectionate friend,*
> *Jenny.*

Deborah lowered the letter to her lap. Richard had evidently been as discreet as he claimed, for if Jenny suspected him of having a ladylove, then she would have mentioned it as confirmation of the unlikelihood of his liaison with Lady Ann. His wish to keep Sabrina out of it all had been granted, but at the same time so had the malevolent wishes of Sir James and Lady Ann.

With sudden resolve Deborah rose from the chair by the fire. Her mind was made up. She would accept Jenny's invitation and go to Bath. If it was possible, she would get to the bottom of it all and restore her brother's honor.

"Amy, we will be leaving for Bath as soon as we can, and I wish you to pack for a stay of several weeks."

The maid's jaw dropped, and she came to the archway of the dressing room to stare incredulously at her mistress.

Deborah nodded. "Yes, Amy, you did hear correctly. We're going to Bath, and we'll be staying at the residence of Mr. and Mrs. Masterson in Royal Crescent. I know that this is the first time in three years that I've decided to go away like this, but if you read this item in the newspaper, you will understand why."

Deborah gave her the newspaper, knowing she could read because she herself had taught her.

Amy read, and her eyes widened. "Oh, madam!" she cried when she'd finished. "Mr. Wexford is too fine a gentleman to ever do such a thing!"

"Thank you for saying that, Amy. Yes, he is, and if I can prove him innocent, I mean to do so. Will you please inform Briggs that I shall shortly be writing a letter to Mrs. Masterson, which I wish a messenger to ride to Bath with immediately."

"Yes, madam."

"And you may tell everyone below stairs the reason for my journey to Bath."

"Yes, madam."

As the door closed behind the maid, Deborah went to the window to look out over the windswept garden and bowling green. A mounted messenger would travel the seventy or so miles to Bath before nightfall, but her carriage would take much longer. The byroads were far from satisfactory at this time of year, and if the weather turned to rain, then traveling would be made even more difficult, but she should be in Bath within a few days.

She found the prospect of emerging into society again rather daunting, for Bath at the height of the season was a hothouse of activity. It was going to be an ordeal for her after so long, but for Richard's sake she would do all she could. How she was going to go about exposing the lies of Sir James Uppingham and Lady Ann Appleby she really didn't know. Perhaps it would all come to naught, but at least she would have done her best.

It was the following morning before the carriage set off from St. Mary Magna. Mercifully the weather was disposed to be kind, although it was still blustery and cold.

Deborah and Amy made themselves as comfortable as possible for the miles ahead. They both wore their warmest traveling clothes and were very glad indeed of the heated bricks wrapped in cloths that had been placed on the floor beneath their feet. Amy was a poor traveler and huddled on the seat opposite her mistress, the hood of her gray woolen cloak pulled up over her head and a lavender pomander in readiness for the inevitable motion sickness.

Deborah gazed nervously out at the last thatched cottage before the road began to climb out of the valley and then curve inland toward the north. In spite of her fur-trimmed gold velvet cloak and warm swansdown muff, she felt cold. She wished Jonathan were with her now, for he would have made her feel so much stronger. She slipped a hand inside her cloak to touch the gold locket around her neck and her unwilling gaze was drawn back to the cliffs above the cove where the *Thetis* had foundered.

No, she mustn't think of the past, for it was the future that was important now—Richard's future. When she reached Bath, she was somehow going to have to speak to Sir James Uppingham and Lady Ann Appleby. They were hardly likely to welcome any approach from Richard Wexford's sister, but maybe at first they wouldn't realize that the Mrs. Marchant who presented her cards to them had anything to do with Richard. It was all she could think of so far, and she still didn't know what she was going to say to them. And then there was the mystery of Sabrina, whoever she was. In her heart of hearts Deborah had the feeling that Richard's secret love held the key to the whole puzzle, although she couldn't think in what way. How could a woman whose connection with Richard wasn't even known to Jenny be the answer to a plot dreamed up by Sir James and Lady Ann?

Deborah's glance moved a little guiltily to the valise she had brought with her for staying overnight at inns on the way. It contained not only her personal possessions, but also Richard's letter and the pocket watch. She bit her lip, for Richard had expressly requested her to keep the timepiece hidden at St. Mary Magna, but intuition told her to bring it with her. She hoped her instincts would not play her false.

It was to prove necessary to stop overnight only once, at the Angel at Sherborne, for the carriage made better progress than expected. By five o'clock the following afternoon they had reached Chippenham, some thirteen miles short of journey's end. Deborah gazed out as they drove through the little market town, and as the houses began to slip away behind, her attention was drawn to some impressive stone gateposts and a cedar-lined drive leading to a handsome redbrick mansion. There was a polished brass nameplate on one of the gateposts—MISS ALGERNON'S ACADEMY FOR THE DAUGHTERS OF GENTLEFOLK.

Deborah did not know it, but the redbrick mansion was to play an important part in the days ahead.

Chapter 3

The carriage breasted the final hill, and at last Bath could be seen spreading up the steep slopes of the valley ahead. The sun was just beginning to sink beyond the horizon as the carriage passed through the turnpike gate on the outskirts of the spa.

Bath was a magnificent sight in the fading afternoon light, a city of clean white stone, with elegant parades, squares, crescents, and terraces. The roads were all laid with even cobbles, and the avenues lined with fine trees which would be in leaf in a month's time. The tower of the medieval abbey rose splendidly in the heart of the town, close to the banks of the beautiful River Avon, and was a reminder that Bath hadn't sprung up entirely because of the fashion for taking the waters, but had been there for many centuries before that. Brighton was fast supplanting it as the most stylish resort, but in March Bath was still the scene of balls, assemblies, routs, masques, and all the other diversions so beloved of high society.

Deborah was relieved that the end of the journey was only minutes away now, but her resolve faltered a little as she looked out of the carriage at the raised pavements and elegant houses. St. Mary Magna suddenly seemed a very long way away.

Amy was also relieved that the journey was nearly over, for the lavender pomander had long since ceased to have any beneficial effect, and the constant swaying of the carriage had been making her feel very ill indeed. She took some comfort from the thought that it would probably be some time before she would be required to undertake the journey home again.

There were few people out and about as the day drew to a close, and the March wind was cold as it blustered through the streets. A lamplighter and his boy were going about their business, trying to finish before darkness fell, and several carriages bowled over the cobbles, conveying their occupants home to their warm houses. But the most common form of transport in Bath was the sedan chair, not only because there were so many invalids in the spa for the sake of their health, but also because there were streets and alleys so steep and narrow that carriages were not always practical.

The road ahead divided into two, the right-hand branch proceeding uphill toward the center of the town, the left-hand branch sweeping down toward the river and the only bridge leading across to the newer part of the city on the far bank. As Deborah's carriage approached the fork, a gentleman driving a scarlet curricle came from the direction of the river, intending to negotiate the corner.

He was very much the tippy with the ribbons and tooled his team of high-stepping grays at such a pace that the feather-light vehicle seemed to skim over the cobbles. He could not help but see the more cumbersome carriage approaching from the other direction, but he was confident of making the turn with several seconds to spare. He reckoned without the coachman's weariness after so many hours on the road. The coachman did not notice the flying curricle, but he did see the uphill climb, and instinctively he urged his team to greater effort, flinging them forward and thus eliminating the precious seconds of leeway upon which the gentleman was depending.

At the last moment the gentleman realized what was happening, and with a loud and very blasphemous curse he managed to rein his team in. The coachman also saw the danger, and as he applied the brakes, both vehicles came to a halt within inches of each other. In the carriage Deborah and Amy were flung sideways as the vehicle lurched to a standstill, and they could hear the coachman's anxious tone as he tried to soothe his rattled team.

The gentleman was beside himself with fury at what he saw as the coachman's recklessness, and after making the curricle's reins fast, he vaulted from the seat and strode purposefully toward the carriage. He was very tall and broad-shouldered and was dressed in the very latest fashion, with an ankle-length charcoal greatcoat that was fitted tightly at his slender waist and highly polished top boots with gilt spurs jingling at the heels. The collar of his greatcoat was turned up, and his top hat was tugged low over his forehead, casting his face in shadow, but the unfortunate coachman did not need to see his face to know that he was enraged.

The gentleman paused by the front of the carriage, his hands on his hips as he looked up. "What in God's name d'you think you're playing at, man? Haven't you any sense at all?" he demanded in a voice that was misleadingly quiet.

The coachman, whose name was Williams, climbed

down reluctantly to face him. "I, er, didn't see you, sir," he admitted unhappily, for he knew that he was the one who was mostly in the wrong.

"Didn't see me? D'you drive with your damned eyes closed?"

This stung Williams a little, for although he should have been more alert, there was no denying that the curricle had been traveling far too fast. "I normally drive with great care, sir, but I have been on the road all day today, and to be honest I did not imagine that anyone would attempt that corner when I was almost upon it myself." It was as close as he dared come to actually accusing the gentleman of sharing the blame, for whoever this toff was, he was most definitely trouble.

The gentleman's voice became icy. "Are you presuming to accuse me of being at fault?" he inquired.

Williams drew wisely back from the brink, for mere coachmen didn't take on swells who were turned out in the best that Bond Street's tailors could supply. Clearing his throat, he lowered his eyes and fell silent.

By now Deborah had recovered from being thrown around in the carriage, and she opened the door to see what had happened. Seeing the curricle and its irate owner, as well as two passing sedan chairs that had halted so that the chairmen could watch the fireworks, she alighted, and she was in time to hear the gentleman's last inquiry. His manner immediately rankled with her, and she walked over to him. "Is something wrong, sir?" she asked coolly.

He removed his tall hat and inclined his head, but his tone was only just civil. "Madam?"

She found herself looking at one of the most handsome and memorable men she had ever encountered.

He was about thirty years old and had a head of thick steely gray hair that was quite astonishing in one so young. His face was lean and refined, and yet rugged and strong at the same time, and his dark-lashed blue eyes were clear and penetrating, but no matter how good-looking he was, his appearance now was spoiled by the disagreeable expression on his face. His whole demeanor left a great deal to be desired, and nothing on earth would have moved her to support his side of any argument.

The way he acknowledged her question made her bridle, and she repeated it in her haughtiest voice. "I asked if something was wrong, sir."

"Yes, madam, something is indeed wrong, for I am not usually given to upbraiding doltish coachmen in public!" he snapped.

"Indeed? It appears to me that ill manners come quite easily to you," she replied. How dared he speak to her like that!

A nerve flickered at his temple. "You are entitled to your opinion on that score, madam," he said frostily.

Her disapproving glance went to his curricle, and she immediately realized what had happened. "You would appear to have overanticipated, sir," she observed, knowing full well that such a statement would provoke him still more. She was not disappointed.

"There would have been ample time had not your oaf decided to increase his speed at the last moment," he replied testily.

"Ample time? Sir, it seems to me that you must have been the one at fault, for you were turning directly into our path. You should have given way."

His blue eyes flashed. "Given way?" he breathed.

"Madam, I have no doubt that under your amazing rules I should have stayed safely at home tonight, and thus permitted you full and sole use of the king's highway!"

"That would indeed have been preferable," she responded, "and it would certainly have been safer for the rest of us."

Somehow he still managed to contain his fury. "May I know who you are, madam?" he inquired.

"My name is Mrs. Marchant."

"Indeed. Well, Mrs. Marchant, I trust I do not have the misfortune to meet you or your fool of a coachman again."

"I trust so, too, Mr., er. . . ?"

"I am the Duke of Gretton."

If the title was meant to impress or intimidate her, it failed, for she was far too angry for that—angry and sufficiently indignant to deliver a broadside. "I confess I am a little surprised to learn that you are a gentleman of such rank, sirrah, for to be sure your conduct is that of a ruffian."

He was goaded. "If we are to stoop to personal insults, madam, let me assure you that I will not hazard a guess as to whether or not you are a lady!"

She was determined to have the last word. "My lord duke, your capacity for guesswork is evidently not to be relied upon at any time," she retorted, casting an insulting glance toward his curricle, and thus implying yet again that she believed his timing and driving to be as atrocious as he.

He did not deign to say anything more but tugged on his hat and then turned to stride away to the curricle. The moment he had resumed his place he flicked the whip and set the startled grays forward at an immediate pace. With a clatter of hooves, they turned the sharp uphill corner, and soon the curricle was skimming away toward Paragon Buildings and the center of the town.

Deborah gazed sourly after him. The Dukedom of Gretton was a proud and ancient one, stretching back to the time of Henry V and Agincourt, but the present holder of the title was quite odious, and she was as hopeful as he that their paths would not cross again.

She turned then to look at Williams. "*Did* you urge your team on at the last moment?" she asked.

"Yes, madam," he confessed uncomfortably, "but I didn't see him, and he was coming like the devil himself!"

"I don't want to hear any more, Williams, just keep your wits about you from now on, for I do not wish to be obliged to defend your skill on every corner in Bath."

"Yes, madam."

He assisted her back into the carriage, and then resumed his place at the reins. As the carriage drove away, the chairmen who had observed the entire incident exchanged glances and raised their eyebrows. Whoever she was, this Mrs. Marchant was a tigress indeed to stand up to the likes of the Duke of Gretton. It wasn't often that the duke came off the worst, but in their opinion he had been bested on this occasion. They grinned at one another and then picked up their chairs to go on their way.

In the carriage Amy's eyes were huge with amazement as she looked at her mistress. It was inconceivable to the maid that her usually shy and quiet employer could square up to a duke in such a way, and it was such a shock that the maid quite forgot her travel sickness.

Deborah was surprised at herself, but something about the Duke of Gretton had provoked her. He was insufferable, and her dislike for him had been immediate and intense. If the incident happened again she was sure she would respond in the same way, and she was glad that she'd put him in his place, but the altercation did not bode well for her stay in Bath, indeed it was a very inauspicious beginning.

The carriage drove past Milsom Street, Bath's most famous and fashionable shopping thoroughfare, and then up through the Circus before driving on to the Royal Crescent, which was acknowledged to be the crowning glory of this city of architectural masterpieces. To be able to boast an address here was a social cachet second to none, and the thirty houses were always taken.

Over five hundred feet in length from end to end, the crescent faced over a wide cobbled carriageway toward an iron railing that separated the road from the downward slope of the open hillside known as Crescent Fields. At the foot of this grassy area, where daffodils bloomed at this time of year, ran the Bath to Bristol highway, and beyond that, one third of a mile distant from the crescent, lay the River Avon. Crescent Fields and the crescent itself were always fashionable places to be seen, but as Deborah's carriage drew up at the curb, there was no one about for darkness had now fallen.

Williams made the reins fast, and then climbed in to go to the door of the Mastersons' house to inform those within that their guest had arrived. Then he returned to open the carriage door in readiness for Deborah to alight. The March wind blew coldly along the pavement, for it was exposed up here above the town.

Jenny's butler, Sanders, hastened out to welcome their guest. He had been with the family for a long time and knew Deborah from the days when she and Jonathan had stayed here. He was a stockily built Hereford man with soft brown eyes, and he wore a plain brown coat, beige breeches, and a powdered wig. He bowed to her. "Welcome to Bath, Mrs. Marchant."

"Thank you, Sanders," she said, accepting his hand and alighting.

"I fear that early today Mr. and Mrs. Masterson were called away because Mr. Masterson's father is gravely ill, but Mrs. McNeil is in residence, and expects you," the butler said.

Deborah was deeply disappointed that she wouldn't see Jenny and Henry, but it would be good to see Jenny's aunt, whose spirited and resourceful outlook on life was a tonic in itself. She paused on the pavement as the butler helped Amy down as well, and then something made her glance along the pavement to the house at the far end of the crescent. There, drawn up at the curb in the full light of a street lamp, was the Duke of Gretton's scarlet curricle. She looked at it in dismay. Please let him be merely calling upon someone, don't let him actually reside here!

She turned quickly to Sanders. "That is the Duke of Gretton's curricle, is it not?"

"Yes, madam. His is the last house. He comes here every year for the season."

Deborah's heart sank, for if the disagreeable duke lived so close, then the possibility of encountering him again was greater than she would have wished. Putting the duke from her mind, she accompanied Sanders out of the dark night and into the warm, brightly lit entrance hall of the house.

Chapter 4

Like many fashionable homes across the land, the Masterson house in Royal Crescent was decorated to resemble the classical architecture of Rome and Greece. The scarcity of marble in England was compensated for by clever and innovative skill with paint and brush, with the result that the walls of the entrance hall appeared to be sheathed in the finest yellow Sienna marble. The floor was flagged with stone, and beyond a graceful white archway there rose a curving staircase. The doors to the basement kitchens and other offices lay out of sight beyond the archway, but closer to were the pedimented white doors of the drawing room and dining room, and everything was illuminated by three patented glass-sided lamps suspended from the decorated ceiling.

Deborah had hardly entered when the drawing room door opened and Mrs. Morag McNeil hastened out. Jenny's aunt was a plump, warm person, with the sort of open countenance that always inspired liking and trust. She had soft hazel eyes and a flawless pink-and-white complexion, and her hair, once a rich brown, was now lavishly powdered to make it a becoming and uniform white. She wore a dove gray taffeta gown and a muslin day bonnet from which lace tippets fluttered as she hurried to greet her guest.

"Deborah, my dear, how delighted I am to see you again at long last, but how sad I am at the circumstances." She spoke with a soft Edinburgh accent, and everything in her manner told of the mixture of pleasure and regret she felt.

Deborah smiled and accepted the older woman's extended hands. "It's good to see you too, Mrs. McNeil."

"Come, we will adjourn directly to the fireside, for we have much to discuss and plan."

"Plan?"

"Why, yes, for our task is quite clear; we are to clear dear Richard's name, and to do that we must devise a suitable stratagem. Come."

Sanders quickly relieved Deborah of her outdoor clothes, and then she followed Mrs. McNeil into the drawing room, leaving Amy and the butler to oversee the two footmen unloading the carriage.

There was rose-pink brocade on the drawing room walls, and a welcoming fire flickered in the hearth of the white marble fireplace. It was an elegant room, with ruched silver silk curtains at the windows that faced over the road toward Crescent Fields. The furniture was upholstered in a rich gray figured velvet, and a glittering chandelier cast a warm light, its droplets flashing now and then in the rising heat from the fire.

Mrs. McNeil ushered Deborah to a comfortable chair close to the hearth, and when they were both seated, she launched immediately into the matter of what had befallen Richard.

"This whole business is monstrous, of course, for

Richard would never perpetrate such a crime, and he certainly wouldn't conduct a liaison with anyone in order to do so. The mere suggestion of an affair of any kind with Lady Ann Appleby is quite ludicrous, for not only is she far too proper and straitlaced for that, but she appears to virtually shun the opposite sex, and her name has certainly never been linked with anyone until now. And it isn't as if she isn't eligible, for as the Earl of Harandon's only daughter, she stands to inherit everything, but she has never married. I am sure that when she passes on, they will find "confirmed spinster" written on her heart. So, you will agree, she is a very unlikely target for any rogue, and least of all for someone as honorable as your brother. Besides, you know his taste; it inclines to delicate little blondes who gaze adoringly at him and make him feel masterful, and Lady Ann is anything but such a creature. She is very strict and conventional, and in looks takes after her Spanish mother, with olive skin, very dark eyes, and straight black hair she wears drawn back in a very tight knot, the better to show off her fine cheek bones. Her constitution isn't very strong, and she is in Bath for the cure. Every day she is to be found in the Pump Room, taking the regulation three glasses of liquid sulphur and iron filings, and she is only ever with a group of other similarly inclined ladies, including me from time to time. The state of her health has been her sole topic of conversation recently, and her physician's word is taken as gospel." Mrs. McNeil sighed. "I once regarded her with considerable affection, but I cannot do that now that she has lent her name to this evil design. I haven't spoken to her since it all came to light and poor Richard was forced to flee in order to escape unfair arrest." Mrs.

McNeil looked regretfully at Deborah. "My dear, he didn't do his cause any favors by taking flight, indeed in many eyes such action merely served to confirm his guilt."

Deborah nodded. "I can well imagine."

"And to think that we knew nothing at all of what was happening. Jenny, Henry, and I had all been to Sydney Gardens to watch a fireworks display, and we returned to the house to be informed by Sanders that Richard and his man had simply packed and left. There was no explanation, merely a verbal apology and an assurance that he was innocent of any misdeeds of which he might be accused. Well, we were shocked, of course, and we became even more shocked when the story began to unravel." Mrs. McNeil sat back in her chair, shaking her head. "Richard would never pay court to any woman in order to steal her jewels, and as to supposedly hiding the stolen item in his carriage! Well, it beggars belief. Sir James Uppingham is a toad of the highest order for saying that he'd seen the necklace there. Not only that, he said he'd witnessed Richard endeavoring to keep the necklace concealed! He and Lady Ann are in it together, I'd stake my reputation upon it, and you and I have to get to the bottom of it and expose them for the criminals they are."

Deborah had to smile a little at the other's vehemence. "That will not be easy."

"No, especially as I have cut them both since this happened. Still, I am certain that my acting talents extend to pretending that I have undergone a change of heart. Yes, I'm quite certain I could carry that off, indeed I would do anything necessary to bring the real culprits to justice."

"I see that you are still as spirited as ever, Mrs. McNeil."

"Oh, indeed, yes, especially when my sense of outrage is aroused, as it is now."

Deborah thought for a moment, and then looked at her again. "How well acquainted are Lady Ann and my brother?"

"Oh, they have only been on nodding terms, I'd stake my reputation upon it. There is absolutely no foundation at all for all this gossip about a liaison, except that Lady Ann herself is declining to either confirm or deny it, which, of course, fuels speculation. They didn't know each other at all until I introduced them about a month ago when Richard first arrived in Bath."

"That's another thing. Why did he come here? When I last saw him he gave me the impression that he would be spending the entire spring at his lodgings in London."

"I don't know why he came, my dear. He just arrived, and of course we put him up, as usual."

"Perhaps he was in pursuit of a fair lady," Deborah murmured, thinking of the mysterious Sabrina.

"I would guess that the very opposite was the case," Mrs. McNeil replied. "In fact, it seems highly probable to me that he left London to come here so that he could *forget* a fair lady."

"Oh? Why do you say that?"

"Because he didn't have a glad eye for anyone while he was here. There didn't seem to be a single pretty face that met with his approval, and he conducted himself as if he was contemplating a monastic life."

Deborah said nothing, for she knew that a monastic existence had been the last thing on her brother's mind.

He had been conducting a clandestine affair with a lady whose family was arranging another match for her, and an elopement had been in the cards as well. Such things did not place Richard Wexford on the side of the monks! If Mrs. McNeil had not observed him admiring the fair sex, it had been because he was so secretly and deeply involved with the enigmatic Sabrina, and no doubt it was that same Sabrina who had brought him to Bath.

Mrs. McNeil's thoughts had returned to Lady Ann Appleby. "Do you know, I'd swear that Richard had never even called upon Lady Ann, let alone seduced her in order to steal her odious diamonds. If that necklace found its way into his carriage, it did so by way of Lady Ann herself, and her accomplice in all this, Sir James Uppingham, with whom, incidentally, she appears not to have any connection at all. Now, *he* and Richard were indeed close friends, at least they were in the beginning, but Richard seemed to change toward him. I recall that a day or so before Richard left Bath, Sir James called upon him here. Richard was at home, but he instructed Sanders to inform Sir James that he was out. I don't know why."

"And so we are no nearer our goal than we were when we first sat down. We don't know why either Lady Ann or Sir James would wish to implement this plot against my brother."

"No, my dear, I fear we aren't, especially as it would appear they do not even know each other. We have no option but to speak to them both, and as I've already said, I am more than capable of pretending to have changed my mind where Richard is concerned. I am prepared to flatter them both that I have seen the error of my ways, and I will beg them to forgive my lack of trust in them. You can come with me, and I will introduce you as my niece's friend, Mrs. Marchant. Marchant isn't all that uncommon a name, and I see no reason why either of them should connect you with Richard. Lady Ann will not know of you, of that I'm sure, but there is a chance that Sir James will be more acquainted with your family, for as I have already said, he and Richard were close friends. However, if I am careful not to mention your first name, or where you are from, then I think he will remain in ignorance.''

''I hope so,'' Deborah replied with feeling.

''Oh, I don't believe there is any problem about actually managing to converse with them; the problem lies in what we are to say that will lead them to unwittingly admit anything.''

''Let us content ourselves in the beginning with simply speaking to them, for at least I will be able to see for myself what they are like.''

''Very well. We can begin first thing in the morning at the Pump Room, where Lady Ann is bound to go as she is following the obligatory regimen. It will be a simple enough matter to engineer a meeting with her there, and even if she is absent for any reason, she and I were friendly enough before for me to call upon her at her residence in Great Pulteney Street. No, Lady Ann does not present a problem, but I fear Sir James may. He and I were never so friendly that I would dream of calling upon him in Queen Square; indeed our meetings were always purely social, either when he called here, or we happened to both attend the same function. He will be at the weekly subscription ball at the Upper Rooms, of course, but that isn't for several days yet.

However, I would guess that he will attend the theater tomorrow night, as will most of Bath.''

''Most of Bath? Why is that?''

''Because the Theatre Royal has made a dazzling coup in acquiring no less an actress than the famous Kate Hatherley. She has been persuaded to desert the London boards for the quainter elegance of Bath, and tomorrow night is her first appearance in one of her most famous roles, Rosalind in *As You Like It*.''

''A coup indeed,'' Deborah murmured. She and Jonathan had once gone to see Kate Hatherley at the Italian Opera House in Covent Garden. On that occasion the actress had been playing the role of her namessake, Kate, in *The Taming of the Shrew*, and she had held the entire audience spellbound with her beauty and brilliance. Kate Hatherley was a vivacious redhead with a voluptuous figure, a beautifully modulated and carrying voice, and the sort of acting talent that is very rare. She was seldom persuaded to leave the capital, where she loved the superior social whirl, and where it was whispered that she was admired by no less a person than the Prince Regent himself. There was a Mr. Hatherley somewhere, but he remained tactfully in the background, and was never with his wife.

Mrs. McNeil drew a long breath. ''*As You Like It* is my favorite Shakespeare play, and I mean to be there. Jenny and Henry have left their private box at my disposal, and you must come too, my dear. A little lighthearted diversion will do you good at such a trying time as this, and if Sir James is there, well, maybe we can manage to speak to him.'' Suddenly something else occurred to her. ''But of course! Why didn't I think of it before! We will be able to find him riding in Sydney Gardens tomorrow afternoon! He is very vain about his horsemanship, and since he has acquired a splendid new Arabian stallion, he has been seen there every day. Gentlemen usually go riding at the same hour in the afternoon, so it will be easy for us to stroll past, and then I can call out to him. Yes, that is what we will do first, and if that fails, then we will try again at the theater in the evening." Mrs. McNeil smiled, and then got up. "My dear, you must forgive me, for I've brought you in here to chitterchatter, when all the time you must be not only weary after your journey but also hungry and thirsty. I will instruct Sanders to serve some tea immediately, and by the time we've sipped a dish or two, I'm sure your maid will have your luggage unpacked and your room in readiness." Pausing for a moment before going to ring the bell for the butler, the older woman put a reassuring hand on Deborah's shoulder. "Don't worry, my dear, between us we'll restore Richard's honor, have no fear of that."

Deborah said nothing, for she felt suddenly very guilty. She hadn't told Mrs. McNeil everything she knew, because Richard had so expressly requested her not to. What would Mrs. McNeil say if she knew that he had not only been secretly seeing the unknown Sabrina, but also that he'd been planning to elope with her?

Chapter 5

The strict rules of taking the Bath cure meant that three glasses of the hot spring water had to be taken every morning at the Pump Room between the hours of eight and nine. Nothing daunted, society had managed to make the occasion into an entertainment, and as a consequence the room was always crowded and noisy. Carriages and sedan chairs choked the surrounding streets and alleys, and the babble of voices carried out into the breezy March air as glass after glass of the restorative but foul-tasting water was served from the steaming fountain inside.

Deborah and Mrs. McNeil elected to use chairs rather than the Masterson town carriage for the brief journey from Royal Crescent, and they alighted by the famous colonnade that gave on to the abbey courtyard and the entrance of the Pump Room.

The two women paused for a moment beneath the colonnade before entering the Pump Room, and Mrs. McNeil leaned closer. ''It is agreed then, I will simply introduce you as Jenny's friend, Mrs. Marchant. I will not mention your first name, nor will I say you are from Dorset. Let us hope that something interesting ensues from this.'' Taking a deep breath, she began to walk briskly toward the door of the Pump Room, and after a moment Deborah followed.

The chamber where the water fountain stood was very splendid and graceful, and decorated harmoniously in pale blue, cream, and gold. At either end were curved recesses, one containing a string quartet playing a Mozart serenade, and the other containing an impressive long-case Tompion clock with a statue of Beau Nash set in a niche in the wall above it. The fountain was situated halfway along one wall, with a counter before it from which a woman was serving glasses of the water, and nearby was another counter with women serving the tea that was necessary to wash away the taste of it. The floor was cluttered with tables and chairs, and it was so crowded that Deborah was daunted as she and Mrs. McNeil paused in the entrance.

The older woman was not in the least put off however. "Come, my dear, we'll circulate, for she is bound to be here somewhere, she always is."

They began to make their way slowly around the room, and after several minutes Deborah was dismayed to find herself staring at a face she had first seen the evening before, and which she did not wish to see again, that of the Duke of Gretton.

He was standing with a large group of ladies and gentlemen near the fountain, and a shaft of pale sunlight fell across his steely gray hair from a window opposite. He wore a corbeau-colored double-breasted coat and tight-fitting cream kerseymere breeches, and there was a diamond pin in the folds of his liberal, unstarched neckcloth. His coat and gray-and-cream-striped marcella waistcoat were only partially buttoned to allow the frills of his cambric shirt to push through, and he was the picture of masculine style and elegance. She had to reluctantly concede that in the cold light of day, he was still as devastatingly handsome as he had appeared the evening before, but even though he was smiling now, she still thought him odious.

She didn't want to go near him, but the path Mrs. McNeil was following would take her within inches of his party. Keeping her eyes lowered so that there would be no chance at all of encountering his gaze, she continued to follow Mrs. McNeil, who was intent upon scanning the entire room for a glimpse of their quarry. If Deborah had glanced up, she would have seen the duke turn to take a glass of the water from the counter to give to one of his companions, but she didn't glance up, and at that very moment someone rose from a table beside her, knocking her so that she in turn jolted the duke's arm. The glass of hot water was spilled all over him, and he gave a stifled oath. Then he recognized her.

"We meet again, madam," he said stiffly.

His tone was warning enough, and she steeled herself for another disagreeable confrontation. "So it would seem, sir," she replied, any thought of apology dying on her lips.

Those in his party had witnessed the accident, but the rest of the room remained unaware, and the babble of conversation and laughter continued all around unabated.

He held Deborah's gaze. "Is it your custom to cause havoc wherever you go? Or do you save your unwelcome attentions solely for me?" he inquired coldly.

She felt her anger rising. If anyone was to blame for

what had happened, it was the person who had risen from the table, which person had now vanished in the crowd. Also, the duke had not take sufficient precautions with the glass, but had turned rather hastily in her opinion. She raised her chin defiantly, ignoring the rest of his party, which was watching the developing contretemps in some bemusement. "Sir, perhaps I should equally inquire whether your attentions are kept just for me? It is hardly my fault if your clumsiness results in a mishap."

"*My* clumsiness?"

"Yes, sirrah, yours."

By now Mrs. McNeil had realized that Deborah was no longer with her and returned in some astonishment to stare at what was happening.

The duke raised a disdainful eyebrow at Deborah. "Madam, your capacity for bending the facts never ceases to amaze me. Tell me, do you mean to make a prolonged stay in Bath? Only I would hate to encounter you on a regular basis, for I doubt if my health is up to it."

"I do not know how long I will be here, sir, but you may rest assured that if I happen to see you anywhere in my vicinity, I will give you a very wide berth indeed, for to be sure you appear to have very little idea of how to proceed without putting others in risk of life and limb!" Deborah was again startled at herself, for to behave like this was totally out of character. She was usually the most even-tempered and reasonable of persons, but something about this insufferable man touched every perverse nerve in her body. She would trade him insult for insult, duke or not!

"*I* have little idea?" he breathed. "Madam, your

47

coachman was gravely at fault yesterday, as I think you know full well.''

"My lord duke, it ill becomes you to blame another for the consequences of your own defective judgment.''

"Indeed? Mrs. Marchant, there is one person above all others who springs to mind when it comes to defective judgment, and that person is *Mr.* Marchant!''

She flinched but still held her ground. "Sirrah, I neither know nor care whether there has been a woman in the land foolish enough to have become your duchess, but somehow I doubt if such a misguided creature exists. I trust that this will be our last encounter.''

He raised his empty glass. "Our last encounter? I'll drink to that.''

Her gray eyes flashed with loathing, and on this occasion she declined to have the last word. With a cool nod of her head, she turned and walked away, followed in a moment by an incredulous Mrs. McNeil, who could not believe the scene she'd just witnessed.

When they were a safe distance away from the Duke of Gretton and his party, Mrs. McNeil seized Deborah's arm and made her turn. "My dear, what on earth was all that about? I had no idea you were even acquainted with the duke.''

"I wish I were not.'' Deborah briefly explained what had happened on her way into Bath the evening before.

Mrs. McNeil was astonished. "I cannot believe that the duke would behave in such a high-handed fashion, for in my experience he has always been the perfect gentleman, and charming as well.''

"He has been neither perfect nor charming in his dealings with me," Deborah replied, casting another dark look in his direction, but his back was toward her now, and a lady in his party was endeavoring unsuccessfully to mop up the water from his coat with her lace-edged handkerchief.

Mrs. McNeil took a long breath. "Well, you stood up for yourself in no uncertain fashion, and no mistake. My dear, I've never seen you in such a tigerish mood."

"That man would try the patience of a saint."

The remark amused Mrs. McNeil. "Deborah, patience did not seem to enter into the proceedings on either side."

"I hope he takes a severe chill from his damp clothes," Deborah went on uncharitably.

"If he does, you may be sure that he will have a very beautiful and attentive nurse to take care of him," Mrs. McNeil observed dryly.

Deborah thought she was referring to the lady who was dabbing his coat with her handkerchief. "Beautiful?" she repeated in surprise, for that was not an adjective that could be applied to someone with such a horsey face and buck teeth.

"Not that lady, I'm referring rather to Kate Hatherley."

Deborah turned to her in astonishment. "The actress? But what has she to do with the duke?"

"You've been in isolation far too long, my dear. Everyone in society knows that Kate is the duke's mistress."

Deborah stared at her. "Really?"

"What reason would I have to invent such a snippet?"

"None at all." Deborah looked toward the duke again. "Well, I confess I'm truly amazed, for I thought Kate Hatherley would show better taste."

"Better taste? My dear Deborah, whatever you may think of Rowan Sinclair, he is still devilishly handsome, very wealthy, of impeccable breeding and lineage, and he is eligible to a fault. You were right to think that he hasn't yet taken a duchess, but that makes him one of the most sought after gentlemen in society."

"But I was under the impression that Mrs. Hatherley was renowned for her gaiety and lightheartedness."

"And so she is."

"Then why on earth has she chosen to favor such a sourshanks as the Duke of Gretton? She must have taken leave of her senses, whether or not he is handsome and wealthy." Deborah despised him so much that she would have no truck with anything said in his defense.

Mrs. McNeil sighed. "I see there is no reasoning with you where he is concerned.

"No, there isn't, for he is beyond the pale."

Mrs. McNeil suddenly glanced past her toward a group of ladies seated around a table. "Those ladies are the ones who usually accompany Lady Ann, but she isn't with them today. I'll just go and inquire after her. You wait here a moment."

After a few moments, she returned. "Well, my dear, it seems that Lady Ann is indisposed and has remained at home today. Come, we'll go there now, and we will be certain to avoid the Duke of Gretton and his party, for I have no desire to witness a repetition of your recent altercation."

"I wouldn't stoop to speak to him again," Deborah said.

Mrs. McNeil pursed her lips. "Indeed? My dear, given the way you feel about him, you wouldn't be able to resist launching in, so I'll keep you out of harm's way. Follow me; we'll go back in a different direction."

The cold air outside made Deborah's breath catch as she and Mrs. McNeil hurried back toward the colonnade and the waiting lines of sedan chairs. Again Mrs. McNeil halted for a moment by the columns. "I trust that Lady Ann will forgive me sufficiently to serve a dish of her excellent China tea, for I am in dire need of refreshment. The wishy-washy brew they serve in the Pump Room isn't excellent, isn't China, and probably isn't even tea."

Deborah smiled. "I recollect from past experience that you are probably correct on all three counts," she said.

Mrs. McNeil glanced back toward the Pump Room entrance. "It seems His Grace of Gretton is departing as well," she murmured.

Deborah couldn't help turning to look. He'd donned a heavy wine red greatcoat and was flexing his fingers as he drew on a pair of tight kid gloves. The light breeze stirred through his striking gray hair, and the blue of his eyes was discernible across the abbey courtyard as he met her gaze. He didn't look away at all, indeed she was the one who did so first, and when she stole another glance a moment later, he was strolling away into the shadows by the abbey.

Mrs. McNeil watched the direction he took. "North Parade, I have no doubt," she murmured.

"North Parade?"

"Kate Hatherley has taken a house there."

"Oh."

Mrs. McNeil turned then and beckoned to the nearest chairmen. "Two chairs for Great Pulteney Street, if you please," she said.

Chapter 6

Great Pulteney Street lay across the river in the newer part of Bath and was approached over Pulteney Bridge, Lady Ann's residence was to be found about halfway along the street on the left, next to a flight of stone steps leading down to the mews lane and the meadows. The house had a blue door with a polished lion's head brass knocker, and it was one of many uniform terrace properties, all of them elegant, and all built of the same handsome Bath stone.

It was customary on calling to send one's cards to the door, but Mrs. McNeil had no intention of allowing Lady Ann to say she was not at home, and so the moment they had alighted from the chairs, she led Deborah purposefully to the blue door and knocked.

A butler answered, and it was clear from his startled expression that he had indeed been given such instructions regarding Lady Ann's former friend. He began to explain that his mistress was not at home, but Mrs. McNeil would have none of it.

"Nonsense, I happen to know that she is in, and since my purpose in coming here is to make my peace with her, I would be obliged if you would convey my felicitations to her and request a few moments of her time. You may inform her that I am aware of having been in the wrong recently and wish to make amends.''

He hesitated.

''Well, go on, man. Do as you are told,'' Mrs. McNeil ordered, waving him away.

He gave up and stood aside for them to enter. Then he went up the staircase, leaving them in the long entrance hall. Mrs. McNeil glanced around at the soothing ice green walls and the delicate pink-and-white tiles on the floor. ''Such elegant taste, do you not agree?'' she murmured, but then something on the floor caught her eye. It was a button, and it lay in a corner where it had rolled unnoticed. Picking it up, she stared at it for a moment but then hastily put it in her reticule as the butler reappeared at the top of the staircase.

''If you will come this way, Lady Ann will receive you,'' he said.

They ascended to the next floor, and Deborah did not have the chance to ask her companion about the button.

Lady Ann Appleby was exactly as Mrs. McNeil had described her and might have been a Spanish infanta instead of the daughter of the very English Earl of Harandon. She was propped up on a mound of lace-trimmed pillows, with a warm cashmere shawl around the shoulders of her frilled white silk nightgown, and in spite of her olive complexion, she looked pale and strained. The volume she had been about to read when her unexpected visitors were announced still lay opened on the coverlet of the bed. It was an edition of the first of Sir Walter Scott's Waverley novels.

Mrs. McNeil waited until the butler had withdrawn, which he did promptly because Lady Ann issued no instructions regarding the serving of tea or any other refreshment, and then she faced the woman in the bed. "Lady Ann, thank you so much for receiving me. Oh, forgive me, allow me to introduce Mrs. Marchant. She is my niece Jenny's good friend and is staying with me at the moment, Jenny and her husband having been called away due to family illness. My dear, this is Lady Ann Appleby."

"Lady Ann." Deborah inclined her head.

"Mrs. Marchant." Lady Ann was evidently not in the least interested in who Mrs. McNeil brought with her, but was very interested indeed in the reason for the call, for her brown eyes went immediately back to her former friend. "What may I do for you, Mrs. McNeil?"

"You may forgive me. I have been sadly in the wrong in this whole business of Mr. Wexford, and I cannot bear it if we remain at odds over it. I should never have doubted your word, I realize that now, but he was a guest in my niece's house, and he seemed everything that was charming and sincere. I was gulled completely, I am ashamed to admit, but now that I have seen the error of my ways, I have come immediately to try to put matters right between us. Can you find it in your heart to forgive me, Lady Ann?"

Deborah marveled at how genuine the apology sounded. Mrs. McNeil was indeed the actress she claimed to be. Perhaps Kate Hatherley should be looking to her laurels!

Lady Ann gave a hesitant smile, and then nodded. "It would please me very much if we were on amicable terms again, Morag, for I have missed our hours over the chess board." She smiled at Deborah. "Mrs. McNeil is a fiendish chess player, Mrs. Marchant, and my advice to you is that you decline any request from her for a game, unless you are a fiend yourself.''

In spite of herself, Deborah found her an oddly sympathetic person. She wanted to despise Lady Ann Appleby, but that was not an easy thing to do.

Lady Ann smiled at Mrs. McNeil. "I'm glad you took the trouble to call, Morag, for it is always disagreeable when one falls out with one's friends."

"I could not agree more. Mrs. Marchant and I went to the Pump Room specifically so that I could speak to you, but then we learned that you were indisposed, and so we came directly here. Lady Ann, I cannot begin to say how sorry I am about everything, but we were all taken in by Mr. Wexford, who is surely the most plausible rogue on earth."

"I would rather not talk about him."

"But—"

"Please, Morag."

Mrs. McNeil was obliged to try another tack. "How glad you must have been to have your necklace returned. I'll warrant you could not thank dear Sir James enough."

"I am not acquainted with Sir James. He took the necklace to the authorities, and they brought it to me."

"You aren't acquainted with him at all?"

"No. We've never even spoken." Lady Ann took a long breath. "Morag, I really would rather not discuss what has happened recently, for I find it all very distressing. Believe me, if I could turn the clock back, I would."

This last was said with such choked emotion that Deborah thought the woman would dissolve into tears. It was a disconcerting moment, for once again it made Lady Ann appear sympathetic.

There was a tap at the door, and the butler entered to inform Lady Ann that her physician had called. There was nothing for it but for Mrs. McNeil and Deborah to leave.

Lady Ann gave a bright smile. "I am not very indisposed, Morag, and will soon be quite well again, I'm sure. Perhaps we could see each other then, and enjoy a game of chess?"

"I look forward to it."

Lady Ann nodded at Deborah. "I am pleased to have met you, Mrs. Marchant."

"And I you, Lady Ann."

"Good day to you both."

"Good day," they replied and withdrew from the room.

They passed the physician on the staircase, and then the butler showed them out. The two chairs had gone, and so they began to walk back toward Pulteney Bridge, beyond which Bath rose splendidly across the hillside with Royal Crescent just visible in the distance.

Mrs. McNeil glanced at Deborah. "Well? What did you think? Can you imagine your brother pursuing her in order to steal her jewels?"

"No."

"Nor I. Oh, I simply don't understand her. I would have accepted that maybe she genuinely believed for some reason that Richard had taken the necklace, but once she let it be believed that he had seduced her first, I knew it was untrue. Now I know even more that she is lying."

"Oh?" Deborah paused, looking inquiringly at her. "Why do you say that?"

"Because it is patently untrue that she and Sir James

57

are unacquainted. I know for a fact that he has called at her house and been admitted.'' Mrs. McNeil opened her reticule and took out the silver button.

Deborah examined it. It was from a gentleman's coat and was beautifully engraved with a heraldic device, a six-spoked cartwheel.

Mrs. McNeil smiled. ''The cartwheel is Sir James Uppingham's badge and is emblazoned on his carriage, his writing paper, his cane, and even upon the saddle of his new horse. His forebears carried it into battle during the Crusades, and he is justifiably proud of it.''

''And you think this is his button?''

''It cannot be anyone else's, for the cartwheel is too exactly his. Do you see how the spokes protrude around the rim? So, Lady Ann cannot be telling the truth when she says she has never even spoken to him. He would not have been admitted if she wasn't there to receive him.''

''But why should she pretend not to know him if she does?''

''Because such a pretense makes their story seem more believable. Why would two perfect strangers concoct a plot against Richard? It might be whispered that two friends or acquaintances could have cause to dislike him sufficiently for some reason or other, but two people who don't know each other? It is a neat touch, I fancy.''

''I find it very difficult to believe any ill of Lady Ann,'' Deborah confessed.

''I promise you you won't find it similarly difficult where Sir James is concerned,'' Mrs. McNeil replied, putting the button back into the reticule. ''When you see him this afternoon in Sydney Gardens, I am sure you will think him the most of a weasel you've ever met. A tall weasel, maybe, but a weasel for all that. I didn't like him when he and Richard were close friends, and I certainly don't like him now. Still, I'm sure my Thespian talents are now sufficiently polished to deceive him as I deceived Lady Ann.''

''Your Thespian talents are nothing short of amazing,'' Deborah replied.

''Yes, they are rather,'' Mrs. McNeil agreed, without any modesty at all. ''I have always fancied myself on the stage, and when we go to the theater tonight, you may be sure that I will be picking Mrs. Hatherley's Rosalind to shreds. Ah, there are some chairs returning from the gardens!''

As two of the chairs were hailed, Deborah glanced back toward Lady Ann's house. There was something about the lady that simply did not add up. But what was it?

Chapter 7

They decided to use the Masterson town carriage that afternoon and set off after a light luncheon. As the carriage drew up outside the Sydney Hotel, Deborah saw that a poster was being nailed to a nearby tree. It announced Kate Hatherley's appearance at the Theatre Royal that night and exhorted all to attend if they wished to see the very finest player in the world.

Except for riders, access to the Sydney Gardens was gained by way of the hotel itself, and Deborah and Mrs. McNeil walked through the building and out into the gardens at the rear. As luck would have it, only one of the rides was in use that day, and it was toward this that the two women made their way, taking up a vantage point by a wide-spreading evergreen to watch the elegant ladies and gentlemen on their glossy mounts. There weren't many ladies, however, for displaying one's equestrian skills in Sydney Gardens was a mainly masculine pursuit.

"What if Sir James decides not to come here today?" Deborah asked, surveying the cavalcade.

"Then there is the theater tonight or the assembly room ball tomorrow, but I feel certain he will be here today. Yes, there he is now! Do you see that gentleman

on the bright chestnut Arabian?—the one with the two
greyhounds following?''

''Yes.''

''That is Sir James Uppingham.''

Deborah stared across at him. He was tall and lean,
and had sandy hair which he chose to wear in rather
exaggerated Apollo curls, but as he turned his horse,
she saw that he did indeed merit being called a weasel,
for he was thin-faced, and his eyes were set close together above his rather pointed nose. He wore a beige
riding coat and white breeches, and he rode at a pace
which best showed off his mount's equine beauty. The
Arabian was indeed worth displaying, for it was one
of the most magnificent horses Deborah had ever seen,
with a shining coat, a beautiful arched neck and dished
head, and, as was the fashion for the breed, its tail
was long and loose, flowing like silk behind it as it
cantered along the broad grass ride. The greyhounds
padded at its heels, all in all giving Sir James every
appearance of being very much a man of fashion and
position.

''I will call him,'' Mrs. McNeil declared, and before Deborah could say anything, that was precisely
what she did. ''Sir James? A moment of your time, I
beg of you.''

He reined in and turned to see who was hailing him,
and there was no smile on his face as he recognized
Mrs. McNeil. It was plain that he had no particular
desire to speak to someone who had been making her
hostility so very clear in recent days.

Mrs. McNeil called again. ''Oh, please, Sir James,
for I do so wish to apologize to you,'' she cried.

Reluctantly he urged his horse toward them, and as
he approached, Deborah saw that his was an inscru-

table, veiled visage. If Lady Ann had confounded her by appearing to be the very opposite of what had been expected, everything about Sir James suggested a devious nature. His eyes were pale and of a color somewhere between hazel and blue, and his lashes were so pale that they were barely visible against his skin. His lips were full and rather sensuous, but they were unsmiling as he reined in before them. He removed his tall hat and inclined his head, but although his manner was civil enough, his eyes remained cold and guarded.

"Madam?" he murmured to Mrs. McNeil, and then his glance slid to Deborah.

Mrs. McNeil quickly introduced her. "Sir James, this is Mrs. Marchant; she is a friend of my niece's and is staying with me for the time being."

"Mrs. Marchant." Her surname did not arouse even a flicker of interest in him.

Deborah inclined her head in reply. "Sir James," she murmured.

Mrs. McNeil cleared her throat uncomfortably. "You must forgive me for accosting you like this, Sir James, but I fear that I have a confession to make."

"A confession?"

"Yes. You see, I have been gravely at fault over Mr. Wexford, and I have already made my peace with Lady Ann, and now I must endeavor to do so with you. I regret being gulled by him, sir, and I now fully accept that he behaved monstrously over the matter of poor Lady Ann's necklace. I would be very grateful if you would accept my sincere apology."

Sir James studied her for a long moment, and then his eyes cleared a little. "Of course I accept your apology, madam." he said graciously.

"Oh, thank you, thank you so much. You don't *know*

how relieved I am." Mrs. McNeil was all smiles, as if a great weight had been lifted from her shoulders. "Shall we see you at the theater tonight, Sir, James?"

"Er, no, Lady Sabrina and I have been invited to dine at Prior Park," he replied.

Deborah's heart had almost stopped within her. Lady Sabrina?

Mrs. McNeil beamed at him. "But of course! How remiss of me to forget to congratulate you upon your betrothal. I wish you and dear Lady Sabrina every happiness in the future."

"Thank you."

"Please say that you will be attending the assembly room ball, for I would so like to extend my congratulations to her in person."

"Yes, we are attending. But for the moment, you must excuse me . . ." His mount was impatient and had been capering about for several seconds.

"Yes, of course. Good day to you, Sir James."

"Good day to you, Mrs. McNeil. Mrs. Marchant." Touching his hat to Deborah, he turned the restive horse away and urged it into a canter.

Deborah stared after him, her mind racing. Lady Sabrina? A betrothal? Surely it had to be Richard's Sabrina!

Mrs. McNeil looked at her in concern. "Is something wrong, my dear?"

"When was Sir James betrothed to Lady Sabrina?" she asked.

"When? Let me see, it was the day after Richard left Bath. Yes, that was when it took place."

"Was it a long-planned contract?"

Mrs. McNeil was puzzled at the questions. "Yes, as

it happens it was. The arrangement was first made by their late fathers. Why do you ask?"

"Mrs. McNeil, who exactly is Lady Sabrina?"

"Lady Sabrina Sinclair, the Duke of Gretton's only sister."

Not the Duke of Gretton again. He seemed to be at every corner!

Mrs. McNeil studied her. "My dear, I trust you are going to explain?"

Deborah nodded. "Yes, but first I must beg you to accept my apologies, for I haven't been as forthcoming with you as I might have been. There are things I haven't said because Richard instructed me not to, but now I think I must tell you everything I know. Please let's walk, for I feel so guilty that I can't just stand here."

"As you wish."

They strolled slowly away from the ride, and Deborah related what had happened when she'd returned from her clifftop ride and found the package waiting for her. When she'd finished she faced Mrs. McNeil. "I cannot believe that Richard's Sabrina and Sir James's Lady Sabrina are two different people. Too many facts tally."

"They do indeed, for Lady Sabrina is everything that Richard would find irresistible. She is small and dainty, with golden hair and the sweetest of natures. He could not help but love her, I'm sure. And what is more, although the match is an arranged one, Sir James has always adored her. For him it isn't a mere contract but a love match. I have often wondered what she thought, and now I know. She didn't want to be betrothed to Sir James because she was in love with Richard, but her brother the duke was for the Uppingham match because he saw it as his filial duty to continue with a contract he knew his father had wished for, and which he quite probably believed met with Sabrina's own approval. She has certainly never given any hint to the contrary.'' Mrs. McNeil drew a long breath. ''How sad that she and Richard felt their only course was to elope.''

''Which they would have done but for the intervention of Sir James and Lady Ann,'' Deborah observed.

''True. Well, we have Sir James's motive, do we not? He must have found out, and I'm sure he would do anything to rid himself of a rival, but I still cannot think why Lady Ann would lend herself to such a despicable scheme.''

''It is Lady Sabrina who is of more interest to me,'' Deborah murmured. ''I must speak to her somehow.''

''My dear, Richard wanted her to be left alone; his letter appears to have made that very clear indeed.''

''I know, but I cannot stand idly by and do nothing. He is my brother and I love him very much, too much to obey him in this. I will not let Sir James and Lady Ann get away with what they've done, nor will I permit Lady Sabrina Sinclair to be safe with her secret if it is at Richard's expense.

''I admire your spirit, my dear, but feel I should point out that if you approach Lady Sabrina, you will have the Duke of Gretton to contend with. He will not suffer any scandal to touch his sister's name, as touch it it will if it gets out that she and Richard were planning an elopement. The Bath gossip-mongers would have a grand time with such a snippet, make no mistake, and the duke would not take kindly to that.''

''Oh, plague take the Duke of Gretton! Would he rather his sister married a villainous rogue than an honorable man like Richard? If that is so, then His Grace of Gretton is more of a toad than I already believe.''

Mrs. McNeil fell silent. With this new revelation of Lady Sabrina's involvement, she sensed that there were considerable storms ahead.

Chapter 8

The gown Deborah chose to wear to the theater that night was made of delicate silver gray silk which brought out the color of her eyes. It was high-waisted, with little puffed sleeves and a low square neckline, and the material was so sheer and clinging that it showed off every curving line of her figure. With it she wore the amethyst necklace and earrings that Jonathan had given her on their wedding day, long white gloves, white silk stockings, and little silver satin slippers that matched the lozenge-shaped reticule looped over her wrist. Her appearance was completed by a knotted silver shawl and a folded ivory fan she wore over the same wrist as the reticule. Amy combed her coal black hair up into a knot from which tumbled several heavy ringlets, and the only adornment to her coiffure was a tiny posy of violets.

It was the first time in three years that she had dressed for such an occasion as this, and as she studied herself in the long cheval glass in the corner of her candlelit bedroom, she found herself remembering times gone by when Jonathan would have come into her room before they left. He would always stand behind her, meeting her eyes in the mirror as he whispered how beautiful she was. Then he would always bend his head to kiss her naked shoulder.

She closed her eyes, conscious of a frisson of pleasure, for the memory was so real that the touch of his lips was almost tangible. But when she opened her eyes again, she wasn't in their room at St. Mary Magna or their London town house in Berkeley Square; instead she was here in Royal Crescent, with all the problems of the present around her.

She turned from the cheval glass and glanced around the room. It was prettily decorated with yellow-and-white-striped Chinese silk on the walls, and a blue carpet on the floor. There was a blue-canopied four-poster bed, a fireside chair upholstered in golden brocade, several wardrobes, and a dressing table that was draped with frilled white muslin. The single tall window faced out over the front of the house, and the fringed yellow velvet curtains were firmly drawn against the chill of the night air outside. It was warm inside, however, with candles and firelight to lend a gently moving glow, and the fragrance of roses was heady from the vial of scent Amy had knocked over a little earlier. The maid was now tidying the dressing table, putting away unused pins, carefully arranging her mistress's silver-handled brushes and combs, and then tidying the Chinese cosmetic box that had provided the rouge on Deborah's lips and cheeks, and the touch of white powder to stop her nose from shining.

A carriage drew up outside, and the maid hurried to look out. "It's time, madam," she said, turning to fetch Deborah's purple velvet evening cloak from the fireside chair, where it had been keeping warm.

With the knotted shawl carefully rolled up and tucked beneath the cloak, Deborah left the bedroom and went downstairs to the hall, where Mrs. McNeil was waiting for her. The older woman wore a scarlet satin cloak that was warmly lined with swansdown, and beneath it she had on an emerald green tunic dress over a simple white silk slip with a black Roman key design around the hem. On her head was a white silk turban with aigrettes fixed to the side, and she wore an emerald necklace.

A few minutes later Sanders closed the carriage door and then nodded to the coachman, and the team strained forward to make the brief journey down through Bath to the Theatre Royal. The route took them through Queen Square, where Sir James Uppingham resided, and Mrs. McNeil pointed out his house, which had green shutters and occupied a pleasant corner position. His carriage was waiting at the door, in readiness to convey him first to Royal Crescent for Lady Sabrina, and then to take them both on to their dinner engagement at Prior Park, a large mansion on the hillside overlooking Bath from the far side of the spa limits. Deborah wished that he and the lady were attending the theater instead, for she dearly wished to see Lady Sabrina Sinclair, who was the cause of so much trouble for Richard.

One of the theater footmen hastened to open the carriage door as Deborah and Mrs. McNeil arrived, and as Deborah was assisted down she was a little daunted by the crush of elegant theatergoers filling the vestibule. The light from a number of chandeliers fell upon the uniforms, decorations, and formal black velvet of the gentlemen, and upon the costly gowns, jewels, plumes, and naked shoulders of the ladies. Fans wafted to and fro, quizzing glasses were raised, and the drawl of polite conversation drifted out as Deborah and Mrs. McNeil mounted the shallow flight of steps and then entered the building.

More footmen came to relieve them of their cloaks and assist with their shawls, and two small boys dressed as Turkish potentates came to give them program sheets. Then they were left to mingle as they chose, or to go directly to their box. They had previously decided upon the latter course, but the staircase was so crowded that progress was virtually impossible, and as they waited for the way to clear a little, Deborah glanced back toward the doorway. She was in time to see the Duke of Gretton enter.

His gray hair was quite startling as he removed the cocked hat that was *de rigueur* for the theater, and then he turned for a footman to divest him of his cloak. Formal evening black became him very well, and his white silk breeches outlined his long legs. His neckcloth was lavishly trimmed with lace, and there was more lace on the front of his shirt and spilling from the cuff of his tightly cut coat. He wore a partially buttoned white satin waistcoat, and there was a diamond pin on the knot of his neckcloth. The pin flashed as he turned back again to accept his cocked hat and tuck it under his arm. He was every inch a distinguished gentleman of elegance and fashion, but one could not judge a book by its cover, for when one opened the volume that was Rowan Sinclair, one found a very disagreeable text indeed.

Suddenly he looked directly toward her, almost as if he felt the close scrutiny to which he was being subjected. With a white-gloved hand he toyed with the lace spilling from his cuff, and then he looked away again. Not by so much as a flicker of his eyes did he acknowledge even recognizing her. She felt dull color flooding into her cheeks, and she too looked away. To her relief the crush on the staircase began to clear, and she and Mrs. McNeil were able to move away from the vestibule toward the auditorium and the private boxes.

The Mastersons' box was placed advantageously near the stage, and its two occupants enjoyed a comfort and space denied to nearly everyone else, for most of the other boxes were filled to capacity.

It was some time before Deborah again noticed the Duke of Gretton. He was in one of the few other almost empty boxes and was lounging back in his chair staring at a point somewhere near the top of the drop curtain. He was lost in thought, and on this occasion did not feel her gaze upon him. She wondered what he was thinking about. Most probably it was the delightful prospect of seeing his mistress.

Two men began to light the lamps along the foot of the stage, and the audience fell silent, settling back expectantly for the curtain to rise. Deborah glanced again at Rowan Sinclair. He wasn't lounging in his chair now but was sitting forward, his attention fully upon the brilliant stage as the curtain rose and *As You Like It* commenced.

Kate Hatherley was as beautiful and talented as Deborah remembered. She had a mane of rich chestnut curls, lustrous hazel eyes, and the sort of presence on stage that most players would have killed for. When she was there she dominated everything, and never had the role of Rosalind been better performed. It wasn't until just before the intermission that Deborah noticed how frequently the actress's warm glance went to her lover in his private box, and as for the duke, his gaze scarcely wavered from his magnificent mistress.

Deborah still harbored uncharitable thoughts where Rowan Sinclair was concerned, and she could not believe that someone as vibrant and full of *joie de vivre* as Kate Hatherley could be enthralled by such an arrogant and impossible man. Evidently he had hidden qualities, but they were so well hidden that in her opinion they were buried beyond all detection!

When it came the intermission was very welcome indeed, for the theater was very hot and many of the audience wished to take advantage of the refreshing drinks provided in the vestibule. Deborah and Mrs. McNeil were no exceptions, for the thought of iced lime cup was very enticing indeed, and so they left their box to make their way down the staircase again. The babble of voices in the vestibule was so loud that it was hard to make oneself heard, and as Deborah left Mrs. McNeil and pushed her way toward the table where the drinks were to be acquired, Rowan Sinclair was the last person on her mind. But she was about to remember him again, and in circumstances as unpleasing as the two other occasions upon which they'd met.

She had almost fought her way to the table when she trod upon the cocked hat dropped by a gentleman to her left. She immediately stooped to retrieve it and brush the dust of her footprint from its pristine black surface, and then she raised her eyes to the gentleman concerned. Her heart sank at the virtual inevitability of finding that it was the Duke of Gretton.

His blue eyes were coolly resigned. "Is there something about my taste in apparel which offends you, Mrs. Marchant?" he inquired, his voice raised in order to be heard above the hubbub.

"Your apparel is of no interest to me, sirrah, but rather is it you yourself that offends me," she replied, not bothering to brush the remaining dust from the hat, but simply thrusting it into his hand.

He glanced down at the unfortunate hat, and then met her gaze again. "Will you grant me one small favor, madam? Please promise me that you will not be attending the next assembly room ball, for if you do I fear we are bound to meet once again, and I shudder to imagine what catastrophe might further befall my innocent clothing."

Her gray eyes flashed. "Sirrah, you alone have been responsible for every mishap that has occurred when you and I have met, and if you are becoming fearful for your sartorial perfection, I suggest that you should be the one to stay away from the ball, not me."

With that she turned her back on him, and proceeded to the table to request two glasses of the lime cup. Then, being very careful to steer well clear of him, she pushed her way back out of the crush to where Mrs. McNeil was waiting.

The older woman had witnessed the latest heated exchange. "Oh, dear, things appear to be going from bad to worse where you and the duke are concerned," she murmured, sipping the deliciously cold drink.

"It was hardly my fault that he dropped his wretched hat."

"No, but if you wish to approach his sister, might it not have been more sensible to adopt a less antagonistic manner?"

Deborah lowered her glance and sighed. "You are right, of course, but it is very difficult to maintain one's temper when one is spoken to as I was a moment ago. "Is there something about my apparel which offends you, Mrs. Marchant?" She mimicked his voice, and then pulled a face.

Mrs. McNeil smiled. "I grant you that such an inquiry was calculated to goad."

"It was indeed," Deborah replied, turning to glance toward him again, but he was nowhere to be seen. "No doubt he's eager to feast his eyes upon his inamorata again," she observed acidly.

"As well he might, for she is very lovely, and, I have to confess, she is also extremely talented. I cannot fault her performance, can you?"

"No."

The bell was ringing to summon everyone back to their seats, and they quickly finished their glasses before rejoining the flow of people on the staircase. Within a few minutes the performance continued, but the latest encounter with the duke had unsettled Deborah so that she took little pleasure in what was left of the evening. She was conscious of his presence across the auditorium, and when she glanced toward him, once or twice she found his gaze upon her. This was even more unsettling, and she was mightily relieved when the curtain was lowered for the last time, and Kate stepped before it to receive the audience's justifiable adulation. She took curtsy after curtsy, and flowers were thrown at her feet as the applause echoed endlessly around the auditorium. When Deborah glanced once more toward Rowan Sinclair's box, she saw that it was empty.

The jam of carriages and sedan chairs outside the theater was quite unbelievable, and it was made far worse because the narrow streets nearby were really unsuitable for large vehicles. It was chilly standing by the steps waiting for their carriage to reach them, and in the end Deborah and Mrs. McNeil could bear it no more but hastened along the lamplit pavement to where they could see their vehicle in the long line that was moving at snails' pace around the square.

They climbed thankfully inside, and as Deborah settled back in her seat, she looked out and saw that they were actually close to the alley that led to the stage door at the rear of the theater. She could see the door, and in the light of the lamp above it she saw a gentleman waiting. The door opened then, and Kate emerged. She wore a white satin cloak with apricot fur trimming, and she smiled at the gentleman, who immediately drew her into his arms and kissed her on the lips. The lamplight fell upon his face, and Deborah stared as she unwillingly observed the skill and passion with which the Duke of Gretton embraced his beautiful mistress. To her unutterable relief the carriage began to move forward, carrying her past the alley so that she couldn't see anything more, and a moment after that the coachman managed to see an opening in the crush ahead and maneuvered the vehicle clear of the crush. Soon he was bringing the team up to a smart trot for the drive back up through the town to Royal Crescent.

As Deborah and Mrs. McNeil alighted at their door, their attention was immediately drawn along the crescent to the last house, where another carriage was just drawing up. Deborah paused, for she recognized the vehicle as being the same one which had earlier been outside Sir James Uppingham's residence in Queen Square. As she watched, Sir James himself climbed quickly down and hastened to the house, where he knocked urgently at the door before hurrying back to the carriage. Light flooded out as the butler opened the door and looked out. Sir James shouted something to him, and the butler hurried out to assist him. They both gently helped a lady down. She was half-swooning, and Sir James had to lift her from her feet to carry her into the house.

Mrs. McNeil had also observed the goings-on at the end of the crescent, and as Sir James carried the lady through the doorway, she caught a glimpse of short golden hair. "It's Lady Sabrina!" she gasped. "Oh, dear, I wonder what on earth is wrong?"

"I pray it is nothing serious, for I *must* speak to her," Deborah replied, staring along the curve of the crescent.

Chapter 9

Unable to sleep for wondering what was happening, Deborah watched from her bedroom window as the doctor hurried past from his residence a few doors away. Sir James's carriage was still by the end house, and the butler waited at the door to admit the doctor. Then the door closed, and all was quiet for a moment before a footman emerged and ran down across Crescent Fields to take the shortest route into the town. Where was he going? Had he been sent to bring the duke from his mistress's house in North Parade?

Deborah lingered by the window and at last heard another carriage approaching. It drove past at speed and drew up behind Sir James's vehicle. The duke alighted and hurried into the house. Another age seemed to pass, and then the house door was opened once more, and Sir James and the doctor emerged. They paused on the doorstep to shake hands with the duke, and by their manner Deborah could tell that all appeared to be well. The doctor hurried home again, and after exchanging a few further words with the duke, Sir James returned to his vehicle and drove away. Deborah saw the duke gesture to his waiting coachman, evidently dismissing him, and as that vehicle also drove slowly away, turning at the end of the crescent to make its way toward the mews, the duke retreated inside the house and closed the door. It seemed he was not returning to Kate's arms tonight. Soon after that the lights of the house were extinguished, and Deborah knew that nothing more would happen. Reassured that nothing was seriously wrong with Lady Sabrina, Deborah at last felt able to retire to her bed, where she fell immediately into a deep sleep.

She slept late the following morning, and the sun was high in the sky when at last Amy came to awaken her with a welcome cup of Mrs. McNeil's favorite China tea. She was soon joined by Mrs. McNeil herself, who sat in a sunny chair by the window and looked out approvingly over the spring scene in Crescent Fields as she too enjoyed her morning tea. Such weather enticed many people out for a stroll, for it was very much the thing to be seen walking in Crescent Fields, where the daffodils nodded in the light breeze, and where this morning a military band was practicing in readiness for a display in a few days' time.

Mrs. McNeil's attention was soon drawn away from what was happening outside as she learned of the night's events after she herself had retired. She turned in the chair and lowered her cup, the folds of her shell-pink woolen wrap parting to reveal the frills on her nightgown as she sat forward intently.

"The duke was sent for, you say?"

"Well, a running footman set off down Crescent Fields, and within half an hour or so the duke's carriage drove back apace."

"But you think Lady Sabrina isn't in any danger?"

"Not judging by the atmosphere when Sir James

and the doctor left. I think she was just taken a little unwell at Prior Park.''

Mrs. McNeil looked at her for a moment, and then returned her attention to what was happening outside. "He drove off a short while ago, did you know?" she inquired.

"No, nor do I care."

"He cuts quite a dash in that curricle; indeed I don't think I've seen a better hand with the ribbons."

Deborah didn't respond. She cordially hoped the curricle would overturn and deposit His Grace of Gretton in something unmentionable, something steaming, smelly, and extremely abundant!

Mrs. McNeil was sipping her cup once more, and suddenly she lowered it with a clatter. "Why, I do believe that Lady Sabrina has just left the house! Yes, it *is* her, and she's taking her dog for a walk in the fields!"

Deborah set her own cup aside and hurried to the window. A young woman in a bluebell-colored cloak with a fur-trimmed hem and hood was crossing toward one of the gates in the iron railings bounding the grassy slope, and a white poodle on a silver lead trotted at her heels. The spring breeze was playful as it breathed over the exposed hillside, and it caught her hood and tugged it momentarily back from her head. In the seconds before she pulled it back into place once more, Deborah saw a sweet heart-shaped face and bright golden curls that were cut modishly short.

Mrs. McNeil glanced up at Deborah. "Well, it's an absolutely ideal opportunity. She is alone, and the duke isn't at home to witness anything from the window. If you hurry . . ."

Deborah had already run to the wardrobe. There

was no time to ring for Amy, and Mrs. McNeil assisted her with her clothes and hair. Within a few minutes she too had emerged into the morning air and was crossing to one of the gates into Crescent Fields.

Most of the people who were strolling on the grassy slope had gathered to listen to the band, but Sabrina paid no attention to the music as she walked the poodle down the slope between the drifts of daffodils. Deborah hastened after her, determined to use the chance to open up a conversation. She knew how she meant to do it, for it would be the simplest thing in the world to make a fuss of the poodle.

Sabrina wasn't walking very quickly, indeed Deborah soon began to notice that she was moving more and more slowly, until at last she came to a halt close to one of the few trees, a silver birch that had yet to come into leaf. For a moment she stood there, and then to Deborah's horror she put a hand up to her forehead and began to sway before crumpling to the grass, the poodle's lead still twined around her fingers.

Deborah was so startled that for a moment she couldn't move. No one else seemed to have noticed what had happened, for all attention was upon the band, and she hesitated for a second or so before running toward the motionless figure on the ground. Kneeling beside her, she looked anxiously into Sabrina's ashen face.

"Lady Sabrina?" she said hesitantly, but there was no response, indeed there was no movement at all.

The poodle whined and nuzzled its mistress's hair, but still she just lay there. Deborah gazed down at her face. Lady Sabrina Sinclair was very lovely indeed, with the sort of doll-like fragility that would have enslaved Richard from the first moment he saw her.

Unknown to Deborah, the duke had been obliged to cut short his drive into Bath, for one of his valuable horses had gone lame, and he was at that moment leading the curricle back along the crescent. He saw his sister collapse, and with a dismayed oath he quickly made the team fast to the railings before leaping over and running down the slope to where Deborah was kneeling anxiously beside her.

He didn't recognize Deborah as he tossed his hat and gloves on to the grass and then crouched down to take one of his sister's hands and rub it in an effort to bring her around. "She's my sister. What happened?" he asked urgently.

"I don't really know. She was walking with the dog, and suddenly she just fainted away," Deborah replied.

He recognized the voice and looked properly at her for the first time. "Yet again, Mrs. Marchant? Fate is making a habit of this."

"I'm sure we can manage to be civil for once," she answered.

"Yes, if we really try, I'm sure you're right," he said, and then looked down at his sister again. He put a hand gently to her cheek. "Can you hear me, sweeting?" he asked, his thumb moving softly against her pale skin.

Sabrina's eyelids fluttered, and she stirred a little.

"Open your eyes, sweeting," he urged.

At last Sabrina looked up at him. Her eyes were as blue as his, but much softer, and for a moment they were confused as she looked past him toward the cloudless sky. She didn't notice Deborah. "What happened?" she whispered. "Why am I lying here?"

"You fainted again, sweeting."

Tears filled her eyes. "Oh, Rowan . . ."

"It's all right, darling, for I'm here with you. Can you sit up?"

"I . . . I think so."

"I'll help you." He pulled her carefully into a sitting position, and the poodle immediately pushed into her arms, licking her face to show how pleased it was that she was apparently herself again after lying so inexplicably asleep in the open air. As she hugged the excited dog, Sabrina noticed Deborah for the first time.

The duke quickly introduced her. "Sabrina, this is Mrs. Marchant. She saw you faint and came to your assistance. Mrs. Marchant, this is my sister, Lady Sabrina Sinclair."

Sabrina smiled. "I'm very grateful to you, Mrs. Marchant."

"It was nothing, Lady Sabrina."

The duke was stern with his sister. "And so you should be grateful, you minx, for you had no business at all coming outside today, not after what happened last night. Dr. Blair expressly forbade—"

"I know, but I wanted to be in the fresh air, and Muffy needed his walk."

"Any of the footmen could have obliged Muffy with his walk, and you were instructed to stay inside until the doctor could call upon you again this afternoon."

"There isn't anything the matter with me, Rowan."

"No? Then why aren't you eating or sleeping, why do you cry in your room all the time, and why do you keep fainting away? It's hardly the conduct of someone who is full of health and strength, is it?"

Sabrina lowered her gaze guiltily, for she knew that further denials would avail her of nothing.

He drew a long breath, and then assumed a more

gentle tone with her. "Do you think you can stand now?"

She nodded, and he reached down to take her hands and pull her carefully to her feet, but as she stood, she immediately began to sway again and he caught her, sweeping her up into his arms. Then he looked apologetically at Deborah.

"I know that I am the last person on earth you would wish to oblige with a favor, Mrs. Marchant, but may I impose by asking you to bring Muffy to the house?" He nodded toward the crescent.

"Of course," she replied.

"Thank you." He smiled at her.

It was one thing to be on the receiving end of his acid tongue, quite another to be exposed to the full force of his charm. Deborah had already been taken aback to realize that there was a warm and tender side to the Duke of Gretton, but the brilliance and clarity of his smile quite demolished her defenses. From having previously found him the end in obnoxiousness, she was suddenly forced to concede that when he wished he could be very winning indeed. Maybe Kate Hatherley's interest in him was understandable after all.

Sabrina linked her arms around his neck as he began to carry her carefully back up the slope, and Deborah paused to retrieve his hat and gloves from the grass before bringing Muffy with her.

All was instant confusion as they reached the house. A footman was immediately despatched to bring the doctor again; a maid hurried up to turn back Sabrina's bed and see that the fire was properly stoked. Another maid was sent to the kitchens for a hot posset, and a further footman was ordered to attend to the curricle, which was still waiting by the railings farther along the crescent.

Sabrina tried to dissuade the duke from sending for the doctor. "I'm truly quite well, Rowan. Please don't send for him again, for I wish to go to the ball tomorrow night."

"You may go provided Dr. Blair says you may."

"Oh, but—"

"That's enough, sweeting, for I won't hear of it unless you are pronounced well." The duke carried her to the staircase at the end of the lofty white-and-gold hall.

Deborah stood in the doorway with Muffy and the duke's hat and gloves. It was clear that in the confusion she'd been forgotten, and so she put the hat and gloves down upon a console table, and then pressed the poodle's lead into the hands of the startled butler.

"Please inform His Grace that I will call upon Lady Sabrina tomorrow to ascertain that she is fully recovered," she said.

"Very well, madam."

As she left the house, she wasn't entirely dissatisfied with the way things had gone. Maybe she hadn't managed to speak properly to Sabrina, but events had conspired to give her the perfect excuse to call again.

She was destined to receive a call herself before then, not from Lady Sabrina, but from Rowan Sinclair himself.

Chapter 10

It was evening, and Deborah sat alone by the fire in the drawing room. Mrs. McNeil had decided to go out to call upon an old friend who had just arrived in Bath, but Deborah had declined to accompany her, preferring instead to spend a few quiet hours reading.

She wore a dark red velvet gown with long sleeves, a square neck, and a gold-buckled belt high beneath her breasts, and her dark hair was brushed loose about her shoulders. Her only jewelry was the gold locket containing Jonathan's portrait, and a volume of Mr. Walpole's *Vathek* lay open on her lap. She read by the light of a four-branched candelabrum, and the only sounds in the room were the ticking of the clock on the mantelshelf and the gentle flutter of the fire as the flames licked around a fresh log.

Vathek was not holding her attention, for her thoughts kept wandering to Richard and his problems. She wondered where he was at this moment. He could not have gone to Wexford Park, because that was the first place the authorities would seek him out, and although the authorities might not know of her or of St. Mary Magna, it was clear that Richard had had no intention in going there, otherwise he would have brought the pocket watch himself rather than risk sending it. Oh, if only he had stayed to face the music, instead of fleeing like a felon, for he had made himself appear so very culpable.

From Richard himself her thoughts inevitably moved on to the three people who had had such a profound effect upon his life, Lady Ann Appleby, Sir James Uppingham, and Lady Sabrina Sinclair. Lady Ann remained something of a paradox, for how could a gentle person such as she appeared to be, be capable of deliberately and cruelly incriminating an innocent man? Sir James, on the other hand, seemed capable of sinking to any depth in order to keep what he regarded as his. As for Lady Sabrina herself . . . Deborah closed the book on her lap. The Duke of Gretton's beautiful sister was bound to have ensnared Richard's soft heart with one glance of her big blue eyes, just as she had obviously ensnared Sir James's heart as well. But Sir James's was a wicked heart, and if Sabrina could only be made to realize the fact . . .

Her hand crept to her locket. She and Jonathan had been blissfully happy during their short time together, and if she could ensure that Richard knew a similar happiness with the woman he loved, and who must still love him, then she would move heaven and earth to bring that about. Slowly she put the volume of *Vathek* on the table beside her chair, and then took the locket from around her neck to gaze fondly at the painted likeness inside.

At that moment she heard a carriage draw up outside, and she glanced at the clock in surprise. Surely Mrs. McNeil could not have returned already, for she had only been gone about an hour. Someone came to the door, and the sound of the knocker echoed through the house. It was a peremptory sound, made by a gentleman rather than a lady.

Sanders went to answer, and she heard the murmur of voices. A moment later the butler came into the drawing room, carrying a small silver salver upon which lay a gentleman's card. As she took it, she saw to her astonishment that it belonged to the Duke of Gretton.

"Very well, Sanders, please show His Grace in here."

"Madam."

The butler withdrew, and then returned to announce the duke. "His Grace, the Duke of Gretton," he said, standing by the door as Rowan Sinclair entered. He wore an indigo corded silk coat and white silk breeches, and a sapphire pin adorned his crisply starched neckcloth. There were frills on the front of his shirt and protruding from his cuffs, and the ghost of a smile touched his lips as he sketched her an elegant bow.

"Mrs. Marchant?"

"My lord."

He waited until Sanders had closed the door again. "This is a most agreeable surprise, Mrs. Marchant, for I did not know that I would find you here. You see, I was somewhat dismayed this morning to find that you had gone without me being able to thank you properly for your assistance. I did not know where to seek you out, and then I recalled that yesterday at the Pump Room and again at the theater, you were with Mrs. McNeil, and so I called here in the hope that she would be able to tell me where I would find you. Instead I was informed that she was out, but that you were at home. I trust you do not mind me calling?"

"Not at all, but there was really no need."

"There was every need."

She felt a little embarrassed. "Please be seated, sir," she said, indicating the seat opposite.

She was very conscious of him as he sat down, as indeed she had been in one way or another since the moment they'd first clashed. It was strange to be exchanging civilities with him like this, and she couldn't help reflecting that his attitude would be very different indeed were he to discover the truth about her presence in Bath. No doubt then he would revert to his former unpleasant self.

She cleared her throat a little. "How is Lady Sabrina now?" she inquired.

"She is well enough, thank you, although she is far from her usual self." He drew a long breath. "Mrs. Marchant, I wish to apologize to you for my disgraceful conduct toward you. I have no real excuse to offer, except that at the time of our first contretemps I was very anxious indeed about Sabrina and was on my way home to see her when the, er, incident occurred. I had been with an, er, acquaintance in North Parade when word was sent to me that she was unwell. The quickest way to Royal Crescent was blocked by an overturned wagon, and I had been forced to make a detour, which is when I almost collided with your carriage. While it does not excuse my behavior, it is all I can offer in mitigation, and I do hope that you are able to forgive me, both for my conduct then, and for my subsequent boorishness. I would very much like to forget that we commenced on such a wrong foot."

"Tempers have been flaring somewhat, haven't they?" She smiled. "I will forgive you, sir, but only provided you forgive me, for I haven't been exactly agreeable myself.''

"You merely retaliated with commendable spirit,'' he said.

Commendable spirit? She had sailed into battle with a vengeance! She glanced away, remembering how provocatively she had responded to his manner during the incident in the street. She was prepared to believe that he had indeed been worried about his sister, but perhaps his anger had also had something to do with having been called away from his mistress in North Parade? She wondered if Kate Hatherley would appreciate being referred to as an acquaintance!

He was thinking of his sister again. "I wish I knew what is wrong with Sabrina, Mrs. Marchant, for she has been so very unwell for the past week or more. Since just before her betrothal, actually. At first I feared that she did not want the match after all, but was afraid to tell me, but she insists that there is nothing she wishes for more than to be married to James. If she truly wishes for the match to proceed, this should be the happiest of times for her, but instead she is so low that she is in a positive decline. I've spoken to the doctor again, but he still insists that she will recover when the spring weather is well and truly with us. The fellow is a buffoon, for it is clear even to me that her condition has nothing to do with the weather!''

No, thought Deborah, but a broken heart would explain it very well indeed.

He sighed. "Before all this she was in excellent spirits, deliriously happy in fact.''

How well it all fitted. She was happy when she and Richard were planning to elope, and she became desperately wretched when she believed herself betrayed by him.

The duke looked at her. "Forgive me, Mrs. Marchant, for my worries are of no concern to you."

"I could tell earlier today that you are exceedingly anxious about Lady Sabrina."

He gave an unexpectedly wry smile. "No doubt you were amazed beyond belief that such a surly bear could be so solicitous."

She lowered her glance. "I do not deny it," she replied frankly.

"I promise you that I am not usually a toad of the first order, and that my ungentlemanly manners have been brought about by anxiety over Sabrina."

"Mrs. McNeil has already spoken in your defense, sir."

"I have an ally?"

"Something of the sort."

He smiled again. "I mean to redeem myself in your eyes from now on."

His smiles were disquieting, and she felt warm color creeping into her cheeks. "You have no need to redeem yourself, sir, for your apologies and explanations have been gladly accepted."

He sat forward. "I'm afraid I do need to continue in this vein, Mrs. Marchant, for I have another favor to beg of you."

"A favor?"

"You left word with my butler that you intend to call upon Sabrina tomorrow. I trust that you still mean to do that?"

"Why, yes." Nothing would keep her away!

"Will you do something for me when you call? If she should say something to you which might give an insight as to why she has been so unwell of late, I do trust with all my heart that you will relay such information to me. I know that it is an imposition, especially as we are barely acquainted, but I am prepared to go to any lengths to see her well and happy again.''

Deborah couldn't meet his eyes in that moment, for she knew only too well what was wrong with his sister. The temptation to tell him was so great that for a second she couldn't trust herself to speak. Now wasn't the time to impart anything of the truth, not until she had had a chance to speak to Sabrina herself.

He misinterpreted her silence. ''It is too much to ask of you. Forgive me.''

''Please, sir, of course it isn't too much to ask. If Lady Sabrina should intimate anything to me, you have my word that I will tell you.''

''I will be eternally grateful.'' He studied her for a moment. ''I seem to recall mentioning the Upper Room ball to you.''

''Yes, I seem to recall that, too,'' she replied, a faint smile touching her lips as she remembered the moment in the theater vestibule.

''I trust that you mean to attend?''

''I am sure I will be there, sir.''

''Then I hope you will reserve a measure for me?''

''You are actually prepared to trust your apparel to such potential calamity?'' she inquired, feigning amazement.

''I am sure my wardrobe is sufficiently well stocked to withstand a few more mishaps. Do I take it then that you will honor me with a dance?''

''If that is your wish, sir.''

''It is my wish. And now I will not encroach upon your time any longer.'' He rose to his feet. ''Thank you again for your assistance today, and for your promise to help me further regarding Sabrina.''

She got up as well, forgetting the locket, which still lay open on her lap. It fell to the carpet, and he immediately bent to retrieve it.

He studied Jonathan's portrait for a moment before returning the locket to her. "Mr. Marchant? Or perhaps I should refer to him as Captain Marchant?''

"Yes.''

"Which vessel does he command?''

Her fingers closed over the locket. "He was the captain of the *Thetis,*" she said quietly, knowing that the ship's name would convey everything to him. The whole of England had been appalled by the disaster that had cost so many lives.

"Mrs. Marchant, I—''

"Please don't say anything, sir,'' she interrupted quickly, guessing that he was thinking of what he'd said to her in the Pump Room. "You were not to know my husband was dead.''

"Nevertheless . . .''

"The entire matter is forgotten, my lord.''

"I will not be able to forget that I said such a very hurtful thing,'' he said quietly, taking her hand and drawing it briefly to his lips. "Contrary to my previous crass observation, Captain Marchant showed great integrity and judgment when he made you his bride.''

Releasing her, he went to the door, but then paused again. "Please feel free to call upon my sister whenever you wish, Mrs. Marchant.''

"Thank you, my lord.''

He met her eyes for a moment more, and then went out into the entrance hall, where Sanders was waiting to attend him. She heard the front door open and his steps as he walked to his carriage. In the few moments before Sanders closed the door again, she heard him issue brief instructions to his coachman. "North Parade, if you please."

"Your Grace."

The door closed, and the sound of the carriage was muffled as it drew away.

Deborah remained where she was. She could still feel the touch of his lips upon her hand, and it was a sensation which made her feel unaccountably vulnerable. It had been so much easier to despise him, for there was safety in hostility.

Chapter 11

Deborah was almost ready to make her call upon Sabrina. Amy was putting the finishing touches to her coiffure, and her gloves, parasol, and reticule lay in readiness upon the dressing table before her. Outside the sun was shining warmly over Bath, and the breeze was so light as to be almost nonexistent. It was a beautiful spring day.

She looked at her reflection in the mirror. She had chosen a short-sleeved white lawn gown with a ruffled collar and an ankle-length hemline that was prettily embroidered with orange and brown flowers. There was a wide brown satin ribbon around the high waistline, and another brown ribbon around the crown of the white chip hat that Amy would soon place carefully over her newly pinned curls. It was so fine outside this morning that she had decided upon a light orange woolen spencer that was left unbuttoned to show off the gown's dainty bodice, and to form a becoming setting for the locket, which was the only jewelry she had decided to wear.

She was nervous as she sat there, for now that she was actually assured of the chance to speak face-to-face with Sabrina, she didn't know how best to bring the conversation around to the true purpose of the visit.

What if Sabrina denied it all? What if she became so distressed that she was taken ill again? What if. . . ? Oh, the possibilities for disaster were legion, and Deborah drew herself up sharply. She must be positive, and not virtually convince herself of failure before she left the house!

The door opened behind her, and Mrs. McNeil came in. She was going shopping in Milsom Street that morning and was ready to leave. Her skirts rustled as she came to the dressing table, meeting Deborah's gaze in the mirror.

"I am about to leave, my dear. I just thought I'd come to wish you well."

"Thank you."

"It will not be easy."

"I know, but I must do it."

Mrs. McNeil nodded. "It should be so simple, a mere fact of convincing her that Richard did not let her down after all, but if she is terrified of scandal and determined to marry Sir James no matter what . . ." Her voice trailed away, and for a moment she was silent. Then she turned to Amy. "Leave us, if you please."

"Madam." Bobbing a swift curtsy, the maid hastened from the room.

Deborah turned inquiringly toward the older woman. "What is it, Mrs. McNeil?"

"My dear, I know that what I am about to say is none of my business and may even be wildly inaccurate, but I feel obliged to say it all the same."

"Say what?"

"Deborah, it concerns the duke. I cannot help but be concerned about your dealings with him."

"My dealings? I don't understand." But an uncomfortable warmth had begun to warm Deborah's cheeks, and she no longer met the other's eyes.

"My dear, in the beginning you could not have disliked him more, indeed, to quote the bard, 'The lady doth protest too much, methinks.' The line between hatred and love is sometimes so faint as to be almost invisible, and since yesterday I fear there is a danger you may cross over that line."

"You could not be more wrong," Deborah declared, getting up and going to the window, but in her heart of hearts she knew the charge was right. Even now she could bring to mind the brush of his lips on her hand and the firmness of his fingers around hers.

Mrs. McNeil studied her. "I hope I am wrong, my dear, for although he is now disposed to be courteous toward you, you must not lose sight of the fact that his liaison with Kate Hatherley is no passing fancy."

"There is no need to be concerned on my behalf, Mrs. McNeil, for although I admit to finding the duke more amiable now, I certainly do not harbor any amorous thoughts about him." You liar, Deborah Marchant, for you wish to know what it would be like to be taken in his arms and kissed with all the rich desire of the kiss you witnessed by the stage door. Telltale color stained Deborah's cheeks so much now that she deliberately kept her face averted, as if she found the spring scene on Crescent Fields completely absorbing.

Mrs. McNeil looked at her for a moment, and then nodded. "I'm relieved to hear it, my dear. Well, I will leave you now. I'll send Amy in again." Turning, she left the room, but outside she paused for a moment, glancing back at the closed door. She wished she could believe Deborah's denials, but she couldn't. Rowan

Sinclair was beyond reach, and only pain lay ahead for any chit foolish enough to fall in love with him.

When Deborah called she was shown through to the conservatory at the rear of the house where Sabrina was taking a cup of chocolate. The conservatory was filled with exotic flowers and climbing plants, and the sunlight shone through a screen of foliage. The air was both earthy and fragrant, and the sound of birdsong echoed around the glass from two canaries in the gilded cage by the door into the gardens. A flower-edged brick path led from the conservatory across the lawns toward the wall of the mews lane, where an open gate afforded a glimpse of the duke as he and a groom examined the lame horse from the curricle team.

As the butler showed Deborah into the conservatory her gaze was immediately drawn toward the scene in the lane. The duke's gray hair was very bright, and he had discarded his coat, revealing the full sleeves and frills of his shirt. His waistcoat was of peacock brocade, and the cut of his white cord breeches was so precise that they might have been molded to his form. Mrs. McNeil's warning echoed in her ears. *You must not lose sight of the fact that his liaison with Kate Hatherley is no passing fancy.*

Sabrina was seated in a small paved area in the middle of the conservatory, where a table and chairs of white-painted wrought iron had been arranged. She wore a high-necked blue sarcenet gown with long sleeves that were puffed at the shoulder and then tightly fitted to the wrists, and a fringed cream cashmere shawl with a bright red-and-black border lay on the table before her, next to the silver tray upon which the chocolate had been served. Muffy was sprawled sleep-ily at her feet but got up immediately as the butler announced Deborah.

"Mrs. Marchant, my lady."

"Thank you, Salter."

He bowed and withdrew.

Sabrina smiled at Deborah. "Please sit down, Mrs. Marchant," she said, leaning down to restrain the poodle, which was trying to jump up to win her guest's attention. "Stop it, Muffy, you know you mustn't do that," she reproved. When Deborah was seated, and Muffy suitably restrained, Sabrina indicated the tray of chocolate. "Would you care to join me, Mrs. Marchant? There is already a spare cup waiting because my brother was supposed to join me, but I fear the stables are more interesting to him than my company."

"Chocolate would be most agreeable, Lady Sabrina."

Sabrina sat forward to pour another cup, and as she handed it to Deborah, she smiled again. "It is most kind of you to show much concern about me, Mrs. Marchant."

"I am only pleased to see you looking a little better this morning."

Sabrina lowered her eyes for a moment. "I am de-termined to overcome my present doldrums, Mrs. Marchant. I have just become betrothed, and I mean to enjoy my betrothal to the full, commencing tonight with the Upper Rooms ball."

"The doctor will permit you to go?"

"Oh, he doesn't think it a good idea, and says it will be too hot and noisy for me, and that if I stay until all hours, it will do me no good at all, but I have insisted upon going. Besides, I promised James that I would be there, and I will keep my promise."

"May I extend my congratulations upon your engagement, Lady Sabrina?"

"Thank you." Sabrina's lovely blue eyes flickered away.

"I wish you and Sir James every happiness."

"Thank you."

Deborah could not help but be conscious of the brevity of the last two responses, or of the lack of enthusiasm. It was all the confirmation she needed that Lady Sabrina Sinclair's heart had not been engaged by the man she had contracted to marry. No matter how fiercely Sir James loved her, his bride-to-be only regarded the betrothal and forthcoming marriage as an arranged match. But how to proceed now?

Deborah was in a quandary, but then Sabrina herself offered the opening by suddenly noticing the locket.

"Why, Mrs. Marchant, what a very charming locket. May I see it?"

"Of course." Deborah put down her cup of chocolate and then removed the locket.

Sabrina examined it. "It's very beautiful. May I be so bold as to ask if I may see inside?"

"Please do."

Sabrina opened the locket, and her lips parted on a smile as she saw the little portrait and the lock of hair. "What a very dashing captain! Is he your husband?"

"Yes." Deborah hesitated, for if Sabrina had been close to Richard, then she was bound to know the significance of Jonathan's name and command. "He is my late husband, Lady Sabrina. Captain Jonathan Marchant of the *Thetis*."

Sabrina's breath caught, and her face drained of all

color as her wide eyes swung alarmedly toward Deborah. "No . . ." she whispered, the locket slipping from her fingers on to the table.

But before Deborah could say anything more, Sir James's cold voice broke into the silence of the conservatory. "Wexford's sister! I should have guessed yesterday!" He strode toward them from the direction of the door into the house, and his pale eyes were bright with anger.

Sabrina was fixed with shock, unable to do or say anything but stare at Deborah as if at a ghost.

Sir James was not similarly stricken however, and his voice shook with fury as he faced Deborah. "So the McNeil woman has seen the error of her ways, has she? She now believes Wexford to be guilty after all and wishes me to forgive her misjudgment? And all the while she neglects to inform me that the woman who is with her is none other than Wexford's sister! What manner of a fool did you take me for?"

Deborah had been taken completely by surprise by his sudden appearance, and his attack momentarily robbed her of the wit to give a suitable response.

His sensuous lips curled unpleasantly. "I don't know what mischief you and that Scottish harridan imagine you can get up to, madam, but I advise you to desist forthwith!"

At last Deborah found her tongue. "Why would you suspect us of anything, sir? Could it be that you have something to hide?"

"How dare you suggest any deceit on my part!" he cried. "Your brother is guilty and has further proved the fact by running away!"

"Many an innocent man has had to flee in order to escape injustice, sir," Deborah replied coldly, her glance moving briefly toward Sabrina, who seemed quite overcome with fear and emotion. Oh, plague take Sir James for arriving when he had. Another few moments, and maybe she would have been able to say the things that really mattered. Now it had all gone wrong, and Sabrina was obviously terrified of exposure.

Sir James's eyes were like flint as he replied to Deborah. "If your brother is the victim of injustice, madam, what reason could there possibly be to accuse him so? Can you answer me that?"

Sabrina gave a choked cry and suddenly rose to her feet. "I wish you would leave immediately, Mrs. Marchant, for I think it despicable of you to insinuate yourself into my society in this fashion. Mr. Wexford is a criminal and a liar, and I bitterly resent your obvious purpose in trying to blacken Sir James and thus probably poor Lady Ann as well."

"Lady Sabrina—"

"Go!" Sabrina's knuckles were white as she clung to the edge of the table, and her whole body quivered like that of a trapped animal. Her eyes were huge with alarm, and it was clear that she thought at any moment her secret would be dragged out into the open.

Sir James was sneeringly triumphant. "Yes, Mrs. Marchant, I think you should go, don't you? Your little stratagem, whatever it is, has failed, and your presence in this house is most definitely not welcome." His glance moved past her then, to the garden, where the duke was returning to the house and would join them in a moment or so.

Deborah saw the glance and turned in dismay.

He entered and paused as he immediately realized something was wrong. "What's going on here?" he asked, his quick gaze moving from one face to the next and coming to rest at last upon his sister, whose distress was only too plain. "Sabrina?"

Her tear-filled eyes met his for only the most fleeting of seconds, and then with a stifled sob she gathered her blue sarcenet skirts and ran from the conservatory, followed by Muffy, whose pattering feet slithered on the paving.

The duke came toward Deborah and Sir James, and his face was very still. "I ask again, what's going on here?" he asked, his tone deceptively even, for it was obvious that he was both troubled and angry that some sort of unpleasant incident had reduced his sister to fresh tears and distress.

Sir James replied first. "This woman is Richard Wexford's sister, and it seems she has come here to try to prove her brother's innocence by accusing me instead. And by accusing Lady Ann as well, of course, that unfortunate lady by definition having to be guilty if I am. Can you imagine it? We are very unlikely accomplices, are we not? We don't even know each other!"

Deborah was stung into anger by this. "If you don't know Lady Ann, why did you call upon her?"

"*Call* on her?" His tone was all innocent incredulity, but his eyes were guarded and alert.

"You dropped a button, sirrah, a silver button with your cartwheel badge engraved upon it!"

"I made no such call, madam."

The duke drew a long breath, and then looked at Deborah. "Mrs. Marchant, *are* you Wexford's sister?"

"Yes."

"And may I presume that Sir James's charge is correct, and your purpose is to prove your brother's innocence?''

Slowly she nodded. "Yes."

"I confess I am disappointed, madam, for your reticence until now would suggest a deviousness which I find disagreeable in the extreme. Given that I have confided in you my concern over my sister, I think it very reprehensible of you to bring your ill will toward Sir James into this house. I would be grateful if in future you stayed well away from my family, madam, and I would be further grateful if you left immediately.''

"As you wish, sir, but may I just point out that you are justifiably protective of Lady Sabrina, as I well understand, so is it not similarly understandable that I should feel the same way about my brother? Richard did not do the things of which he stands accused, and if I can prove that fact, then I will.'' She turned to face Sir James. "You and Lady Ann have conspired against Richard, sirrah, and I will expose you both for the vile liars that you are.'' With her head held high she walked from the conservatory.

But there were tears in her eyes as she emerged into the daylight outside. What a miserable failure it had all been, for she had not only failed to achieve anything in Richard's favor, but had also fallen foul of both the duke and his sister. Fighting the tears back, she walked quickly along the pavement. She wouldn't give up, she wouldn't! This wasn't the end of it, for it was still possible to make Sabrina understand the truth. Maybe she wouldn't willingly agree to speak to the woman she now knew to be Richard's sister, but perhaps she could be coerced into it. The pocket watch with its illuminating inscription might be the very lever, and its existence was something of which the lady would have to be reminded.

No matter what the opposition and difficulty she would encounter, she meant to attend tonight's ball at the Upper Rooms, and somehow or other she would steal an opportunity to point out to Sabrina that her brother might find the watch very interesting indeed. It wasn't fair or kind, but then neither was what was being done to Richard!

It wasn't until she reached the door of the Masterson house that she realized her locket remained on the table in the conservatory, where it had fallen from Sabrina's shocked fingers.

Chapter 12

When Mrs. McNeil was told how badly everything had gone, she was emphatically opposed to any notion of either of them attending the ball that evening. She felt that nothing could now be gained by trying to approach Sabrina, whom she believed would anyway stay at home after being so upset, and she advised Deborah to stay away herself. In her opinion they would have to think of some other way of exposing the real culprits in the business of the stolen necklace.

At first Deborah tried to bring the older woman around, but it soon became clear that nothing would persuade Mrs. McNeil to change her mind. Accepting such implacability was one thing however, but abiding by such advice quite another, and when an invitation arrived that afternoon requesting Mrs. McNeil's presence at a last-minute dinner party, Deborah decided to attend the ball.

None the wiser, Mrs. McNeil set off at eight o'clock in the town carriage, and Deborah repaired immediately to her room to prepare for the ball. With the town carriage already in use, it would be necessary to take a sedan chair to the Upper Rooms, and so a footman was despatched to order one for half past ten, by which time she would know whether or not Sabrina had abided by her declared intention to attend the ball no matter what. Amy watched from the window until the duke's carriage was brought to the front of his house, and then she called Deborah.

"The duke is about to go out, madam," she said.

Deborah hurried to the window and peeped out as well. After a moment the duke emerged looking very distinguished and impressive in the evening black he would require for an occasion like a ball. He paused on the doorstep, and then turned, extending his hand, and a moment later Sabrina emerged as well, enveloped in a pale-green cloak, which parted as she walked to reveal a chestnut silk gown beneath. The duke assisted his sister into the carriage, and then climbed in after her. Within seconds the carriage drew away, coming up to a smart trot as it passed Deborah's window. She and Amy drew discreetly back out of sight, not wishing to be glimpsed against the light in the room. As the sound of the carriage dwindled away into the night, Deborah went to sit before the dressing table for Amy to begin brushing her hair.

When the chairmen knocked at the door at half past ten, Deborah was ready to leave. She wore a primrose satin gown with a very low square neckline, petal sleeves, and an intricately vandyked hem, and pearls trembled from her ears. Her coal black hair was plaited and coiled at the back of her head with soft curls framing her face, and the coiffure was adorned with a padded fillet made of the same primrose satin as the gown. The fillet was twisted with strings of pearls and was finished with a silver tassel that fell to her right shoulder. She carried a fan and a reticule, and over everything she wore the purple velvet cloak she'd worn to the theater two evenings before. Two evenings? Was that all it had been? It seemed an age away now, and it seemed a positive lifetime since that windswept day she had ridden up on to the cliffs near St. Mary Magna, but it had been only six days ago. As the chair conveyed her toward her destination, she steeled herself to achieve her aim tonight. Nothing was going to deflect her on this occasion; somehow she was going to persuade Lady Sabrina Sinclair that she should hear the truth.

The Upper Rooms were so called because they were situated in the upper part of the town, close to the Circus, and they included not only the famous ballroom, but also a tea room, a card room, and the room known as the octagon, which lay in the heart of the building, from which access was gained into the other chambers.

There was an inevitable crush as the chairmen approached the building, for the weekly subscription balls were practically *de rigueur* for society, although there were those who shunned them, as did many in Mrs. McNeil's circle of friends, hence the dinner party arranged on the same night. The entrance to the rooms was brilliantly illuminated, and since a ball was not considered a success unless it was adorned with as many flowers as possible, decorative baskets of spring blooms had been arranged by the doorway.

Deborah alighted from the chair and then hurried inside from the chill of the night. She paused only long enough for a footman to take her cloak, and then she went into the octagon to begin her search. There were dazzling chandeliers, floral arrangements heavy with fragrance, and everywhere a crush of people. The music from the ballroom was almost drowned in the drone of voices, and as Deborah gazed around at all the faces, she was daunted at the prospect of even being able to find Sabrina, let alone talk to her.

She commenced with the tea room, which was large and lofty, with a fine stone screen at one end, supporting an elegant gallery. Every table was filled and there were many people simply perambulating, for it was the thing to be seen strolling around, and so Deborah joined them, her eyes constantly scanning the room in case Sabrina should be present.

It took some time to circulate the entire room, and when she reached the door again she was certain that Sabrina must be elsewhere. The obvious place was the ballroom itself, but she felt she must search the card room first, just in case the duke was there, and his sister was watching him play. She went through the octagon, and then into the card room, which lay at the rear of the building. Here the tables were covered with green baize, and patent lamps on long chains were suspended low over them, casting soft pools of light. It was a peculiarly quiet place, for the playing of cards required concentration, and the ladies and gentlemen indulging in their passion did not do so lightly.

Again Deborah drew blank, for there was no sign of Sabrina or the duke, or indeed of Sir James, which left only the ballroom. A polonaise was playing as she paused for a moment by the entrance, gazing at the elegant scene within. The blue-and-gold chamber was over a hundred feet long and nearly fifty feet wide, and the floor was surrounded by tiers of crimson sofas from where the dancing could be observed in comfort. The windows were placed high in the walls for privacy, and the orchestra played from an apse in the wall opposite them. Five huge chandeliers lit the proceedings, and the master of ceremonies was preparing to announce the next measure as the polonaise drew toward its close.

From the doorway it was very difficult to see everything properly, and Deborah cast around for a place on a sofa in one of the upper tiers. As luck would have it, one was vacated at that moment by a lady and gentleman intending to participate in the next dance, a minuet.

It was very hot in the ballroom, and as she took her seat she snapped open her fan. The floor was crowded as the long sets began to form for the minuet. Jewels winked and flashed, and the ladies' rich gowns were the perfect foil for the more somber tones of the gentlemen's clothes. The master of ceremonies fussed around, finding partners for those who wished to dance but had no one with whom to do so, and then at last the orchestra began to play, and the minuet commenced.

Deborah gazed over the room, searching it foot by foot, tier by tier, and then, quite suddenly, she saw Sir James. His Apollo curls looked as contrived as ever as he stood by one of the lowermost sofas directly opposite where Deborah was seated, and a quizzing glass swung idly in his hand. He looked quite elegant, although in her opinion his neckcloth was just a little too voluminous for good taste. His coat was made of a very fine black figured velvet, and his breeches and stockings revealed him to have surprisingly well-shaped calves for one who was otherwise so thin.

He moved aside slightly, and then she saw Sabrina. She was seated on the sofa, her eyes lowered as she toyed with her closed fan. Her chestnut silk gown was sprinkled with glittering golden embroidery, and there was a plain golden circlet around her forehead, with a tall white plume springing from the back. A gold lace shawl was draped over her arms and there were golden Roman sandals on her feet. Her face was pale and strained, and it was evidently with a great effort that she was paying attention to whatever it was her husband-to-be was saying. She seemed distracted, Deborah thought, as well she might be under the circumstances.

As she watched an elderly lady in silver lace and diamonds came to speak to Sir James. He leaned close to hear her, and then nodded, before briefly drawing Sabrina's hand to his lips and then accompanying the other lady around the edge of the ballroom to a group at another sofa, where he was presented to a military gentleman of some age and importance. Deborah's eyes flew back to the sofa, where Sabrina was now all alone. There was no sign at all of the duke, and no sign of anyone going to join her. It was a chance not to be missed.

Deborah rose swiftly from her place and made her way down to the floor of the ballroom. There was such a crush around the edge of the room that she could only make very slow progress to where Sabrina was seated, and the minuet was coming to an end as at last she had the sofa in sight. Sabrina remained there on her own, with still no sign of the duke or of Sir James returning to join her.

The floor was clearing, and the master of ceremonies announced a *ländler,* but Deborah hardly heard him as she pushed her way through another small crush of people toward the sofa. Then, just as she was about to approach Sabrina, who hadn't yet noticed her, someone caught her arm and made her turn sharply.

"I would prefer it if you did not carry out your intention, Mrs. Marchant,'' said the duke, his blue eyes angry as they looked into hers.

"Please unhand me, sir,'' she requested, unutterably disappointed to have been caught so close to her goal.

"I seem to recall that you promised me a measure tonight,'' he said, still holding her arm.

She stared at him. "I hardly think . . .''

"A promise is a promise, Mrs. Marchant, and I am sure that a *ländler* would be most agreeable.''

She found herself being virtually propelled on to the floor, where he was able to take her by both arms, because that was what the dance required. The *ländler* was perhaps the most intimate of all the fashionable dances, with couples facing each other, arms entwined, rather than forming sets or columns. It was also a leisurely dance, affording the dancers much intimacy and opportunity to talk as they moved, and Deborah felt completely at his mercy as the orchestra struck up the first note, and they began to dance. She also felt at the mercy of her senses, which came to treacherous life at his touch.

He was quiet for a moment, and then caught her unwilling eyes. "Your purpose a moment ago was disagreeably clear to me, Mrs. Marchant. You were about to disobey my orders and speak to my sister again, weren't you?''

"Disobey your *orders*?'' she repeated incredulously. "Sir, this is the nineteenth century, not the thirteenth, and the days are long since gone when the wishes of a duke were law. I am not obliged to do as you say, simply because you say it, and you have no right at all to—''

"Madam, I have every right. You upset Sabrina earlier today, and since she is so delicate at the moment, it falls upon me to do all I can to protect her. She doesn't want to talk to you, she made that quite plain, and so I think it most insensitive and selfish of you to persist in this. I do not find fault with your loyalty to your brother, indeed I find it quite laudable, but I will not have your private problems impinging upon my sister's well-being. Is that clear?''

"If your sister's well-being is of paramount importance in all this, sir, I suggest that you do something to put an end to her match with Sir James Uppingham. *He* is the guilty one, he and Lady Ann Appleby, and I will not stand idly by and let my brother's good name be besmirched because of their scheming.''

"And do you have proof of their guilt?" he demanded coldly.

She looked away. "Not exactly."

"Then I suggest you keep your own counsel until you do. Mrs. Marchant, I do not like being continually at odds with you, but you are leaving me precious little choice. Sir James is to marry my sister, and he has categorically denied any involvement in this whole sorry business, save the fact that he saw the stolen necklace in your brother's carriage. What possible reason could he have for inventing such a tale? Let us face the fact that you have absolutely nothing of any significance to say, and that your purpose is simply to cause as much trouble as you possibly can in order to draw attention away from your brother. Continue, by all means, if that is your pleasure, but do not embroil those close to me. Do I make myself clear?''

"Oh, you make yourself eminently clear, sir," she replied, dull color marking her cheeks.

"I trust that you will take heed from now on."

Her gray eyes moved intently to his face. "Will you promise me one thing, my lord?"

"I fail to see what promise I should extend to you, Mrs. Marchant."

"If I were to find proof of my claims, would you be prepared to listen to me then?"

"I trust you do not mean to fabricate evidence to support your tale?"

"Others have already fabricated evidence, sir, but I will never stoop to that," she replied coolly.

"I have to concede that your tenacity is quite impressive, madam."

"I am driven by a determination to see justice done, sir, and it will not be done until Richard's honor is restored, and until he and . . ." She broke off, for she had been about to mention Sabrina.

"Do go on, Mrs. Marchant, for I am sure you were about to say something interesting."

"I have nothing more to tell for the present, sir, but you have still to say whether or not you will be prepared to consider actual proof of what I say concerning Sir James and Lady Ann."

"It costs me nothing at all to promise to hear you out, Mrs. Marchant, for I know full well that you will never produce anything like proper evidence."

"You are wrong, sir," she answered, but deep inside she feared he might be right. So much depended upon whether Sabrina could be persuaded to help, and so far it was proving impossible to get anywhere near her.

He spoke again. "By the way, it has come to my notice that you left your locket behind this morning. I will see that it is returned."

"Thank you." Her tone was stiff.

"Mrs. Marchant, I really don't enjoy this, you know, but your conduct has made it impossible for me to be more gracious."

She halted then, disengaging her arms from his in the middle of the floor. "My lord duke, I assure you that I will not lose any sleep at all at the thought of your lack of enjoyment. And now, I rather think that we have nothing more to say to each other." Inclining her head, she turned and walked away, threading her path through the circulating dancers. She was shaking inside, not only because she was being continually frustrated in her purpose, but also because she wished with all her heart that she and Rowan Sinclair were on the much more agreeable terms they had been the night before. But that had gone forever now, and he viewed her with suspicion and virtual dislike.

She caught a glimpse of Sabrina's sofa. Sir James had returned to her now and was seated with her, his white-gloved hand tenderly enclosing hers. It was a sight that was guaranteed to spur Deborah to greater effort. She wouldn't give in, not even now! She went back toward her own sofa, but it had been taken and so she lingered by the door for a moment, trying to think of what to do next. Suddenly she noticed a footman walk past with a folded note on a silver tray. He took the note to a gentleman nearby, giving it to him most discreetly. The gentleman opened the piece of paper after turning away to conceal its contents, then he nodded at the footman and followed him from the ballroom. Deborah's eyes lightened. Could a similar note be given to Sabrina?

With sudden resolve she hurried into the octagon, and then into the card room, where small pads of writing paper were kept for use at the tables. Taking one, she adjourned to a corner where one of the tables had just been vacated. A pencil lay on the green baize, amid the cards and dice, and she thought for a moment before picking it up and drawing a recognizable likeness of the pocket watch. Then she carefully folded it and beckoned to a footman.

"Would you take this to Lady Sabrina Sinclair, and tell her where she will find me? She is seated on one of the lowermost sofas directly opposite the entrance to the ballroom. Please be very discreet, for no one else must know." She took a coin from her reticule and pressed it into his hand.

He gave a quick bow. "I will do as you ask, madam," he said, and then he hurried away.

Minutes passed, and just as she was beginning to fear that this ploy had also failed, he returned.

"Madam, her ladyship says that she has an appointment at two o'clock tomorrow with her dressmaker, Madam Beauclerc of Milsom Street, and that she will speak to you then if you wish."

"Thank you." A surge of triumph uplifted Deborah. It had worked! The thought of the watch with its telltale message had forced Sabrina's hand.

Chapter 13

It was not long after this that the master of ceremonies realized that he had a very famous lady singer among his guests. Madame Theodora Callini, a large dowager of impressive dignity, had sung before all the courts of Europe, for the politics of war did not affect those as musically renowned as she, and her presence at the Upper Rooms, Bath, simply could not be allowed to pass unmarked. The master of ceremonies begged and pleaded, even going down on his knee to her, and at last she graciously consented to sing for the gathering.

Word traveled through the rooms like wildfire, and almost everyone adjourned to the ballroom, save those at various tables in the card room whose passion for the turn of a card or the roll of dice by far overwhelmed their appreciation for music. The ballroom thus became an even worse press than before as people jostled for the most advantageous positions beneath the orchestra's apse, where Madame Callini soon appeared. Her first choice of song could not have pleased her audience more, for at this time of seemingly endless war with Napoleon's France "Rule Britannia" appealed to everyone's patriotic pride and fervor.

As the stirring notes rang out over a suddenly quiet room, Sabrina whispered to her brother that she was finding everything far too hot and stuffy, and that she very much wished to go home. The truth of it was that the ball itself had nothing to do with her decision, for she had simply happened to glance toward the doorway into the octagon and had briefly observed Deborah standing there. Seeing Richard's sister had driven home to her the delicacy of her position, and the danger of imminent scandal should her dalliance with him become common knowledge, and suddenly she wished to escape from such a public place and retreat to the safety of home.

Sir James was with them when she made her request of the duke, and he accompanied them from the ballroom to the main entrance of the rooms, where a footman was despatched to call their carriage to the door. Deborah had drawn discreetly out of sight behind a heavy velvet curtain beside the card room entrance as she saw them leaving the ballroom, and the absence of general noise and chatter enabled her to hear what Sabrina was saying as they passed.

"Please don't start worrying about me again, Rowan, for it's simply that it's a little too hot and crowded here after all, but there is no reason whatsoever why I should not still accompany James to the military display tomorrow.

Sir James was anxious. "If you feel in any way unwell between now and then, you must promise me you will send for the doctor again."

Sabrina gave a fleeting smile. "There is no need for that, I assure you," she said quickly. "I am truly looking forward to watching the display on Claverton Down tomorrow morning, and I will be ready at nine."

"But—"

The duke could not entirely disguise his irritation. "Have done with it, James. If Sabrina has had enough of tonight, then that is sufficient reason for me to escort her home. Besides, I cannot abide warbling contraltos who seem to become louder the longer they sing."

Sabrina gave him a sly look. "And besides again, there is another lady whom you wish to see tonight, is there not?" she murmured, and then they all three passed on toward the main entrance and out of Deborah's hearing.

She remained in her hiding place as the duke's carriage pulled up outside, and he assisted Sabrina inside before climbing in after her. Sir James watched them drive away, and then turned back into the rooms, but as he did so he saw something which made him halt, his expression a mixture of surprise and anger. He seemed to be looking directly at Deborah's hiding place behind the curtain, and for a dreadful moment she thought he'd realized she was there, but then it became clear he was looking just to one side of her at the entrance of the card room, where someone she couldn't see was standing facing him.

He glanced around uneasily, and then came closer. "I didn't think you were well enough to attend tonight, madam," he said, his tone outwardly one of polite concern, but his eyes revealing that he was suddenly very much on his guard.

"I'm not well enough, but I must talk to you."

It was Lady Ann Appleby! Deborah pressed back against the wall, trying to see both of them, but only Sir James was in view.

He was pale and angry. "Talk to me? Are you mad?

Why didn't you simply send a message, instead of coming to a place as public as this?''

"I have had enough of it all, and am at the end of my tether. I will no longer do your bidding, and I mean to—''

"Have you taken complete leave of your senses?'' he breathed, glancing around again in case someone should suddenly lose interest in Madame Callini and leave the ballroom. He wasn't concerned about those in the card room, whose concentration upon their own business was absolute.

"I cannot go on,'' Lady Ann replied, her voice shaking with pent-up emotion. "You have forced me into all this, and I cannot bear the guilt a moment longer.''

"You will do as I wish, madam!'' he snapped, still managing to keep his voice low. "I will not discuss it now but will come to your house in an hour's time. I suggest you await me there. I also suggest that you would do well to bear Chippenham in mind.'' This last was uttered with almost tangible menace.

Lady Ann gave a sharp intake of breath. "How did you find out?'' she whispered.

"It is of no consequence, madam, suffice it that I know where to find her.''

"You wouldn't harm her!''

"That is in your hands, Lady Ann. Just give it all a suitable amount of careful thought before you pronounce once and for all that you do not intend to support my wishes any longer. Go home now, and I will join you in an hour's time. I will come to the mews lane as usual.'' Turning on his heel he walked swiftly away into the ballroom, where Madame Callini's rendition of ''Rule Britannia'' was coming to an end, and rapturous applause broke out.

Deborah stayed perfectly still, and after a moment she saw Lady Ann's tall figure hasten toward the main entrance, where she briefly instructed a footman to send for her carriage. Deborah peeped out from behind the curtain and saw how pale and agitated the woman was. She was dressed in a gleaming mauve silk gown with lace sleeves, and a tall white plume sprang from her hair. Everything about her suggested that she was screwed up to an absolute pitch of nerves and anxiety.

Deborah felt a reluctant sympathy for her, for at least she now knew why something about Lady Ann had not added up. Far from being an eager accomplice in the plot against Richard, Lady Ann Appleby was involved against her will. *You have forced me into all this, and I cannot bear the guilt a moment longer.* And of what significance was Chippenham in the scheme of things?

Lady Ann's carriage arrived at the entrance, and the footman brought her cloak and then assisted her out to the waiting vehicle, which a moment later pulled away. Deborah came out from her hiding place, her mind racing. In an hour's time Sir James Uppingham and his unwilling co-conspirator would be closeted together at the house in Great Pulteney Street. If nothing else, surely their presence together in the small hours of the night would raise questions in the minds of those who had hitherto accepted their word in the Richard Wexford affair? If Sir James and Lady Ann were not even social acquaintances, why on earth would he call upon her at such a time? And why would he arrive secretly by way of the mews lane, rather than go openly to the front? Maybe the wrong conclusion would be reached by anyone faced with such facts, but at least it would become clear that things weren't quite as Sir James and Lady Ann had hitherto been pretending.

Deborah knew she had to do something. But what? Suddenly she thought of the duke and his promise to listen to her should she uncover any proper proof to support her side of the story. This clandestine middle-of-the-night might not prove Richard's innocence, but it would certainly prove that Rowan Sinclair's future brother-in-law was up to something.

Hurrying to the entrance, she requested the footman to bring her cloak and then to summon a chair. Two minutes later she was being conveyed back toward Royal Crescent, but as the chair reached the Circus, she was just in time to see the duke's carriage driving out from the far side. He had taken Sabrina home, and was now on his way to see his mistress, just as his sister had slyly implied at the Upper Rooms.

Deborah tapped on the glass of the chair, and the men lowered it to the ground. She opened the front and looked out urgently. "Do you know Kate Hatherley's house in North Parade?" she asked.

The first man nodded. "Yes, ma'am, we do," he replied.

"Take me there, if you please."

"Yes, ma'am," he said, exchanging a glance with his companion. Why would a fine lady such as this wish to call upon an actress? And at such an hour?

Deborah closed the front of the chair again and sat back as the men lifted it to convey her across the wide cobbled area in the center of the Circus, and then down into Gay Street, where the duke's carriage had already vanished from sight.

North Parade was situated beyond the abbey on a slope overlooking the river toward Pulteney Bridge and the newer part of Bath. It was a wide area of pavings, bounded from the slope by a stone balustrade, and the land which swept down to the riverbank was an area of trees, grass, and paths. Bath's first assembly rooms were to be found here, known, naturally enough, as the Lower Rooms, and although still used, they were much smaller and less fashionable than the Upper Rooms. If the original assembly rooms were no longer quite the thing however, the same could not be said of North Parade itself, which was a stylish, sought-after address of elegant three-story town houses, the central one of which boasted a handsome pediment.

Kate Hatherley had taken one of the properties closest to the river, and the duke's carriage was still drawn up at the door as Deborah's chair was at last carried over the pavings after the half-mile long descent through the almost deserted town. The men lowered the chair to the ground, and Deborah stepped out, pausing to hand them a few coins, but as she glanced toward Kate's house, her nerve almost failed her. It was a very shocking thing to call upon a gentleman when he was engaged with his mistress, but was now the time to observe the niceties of every propriety? Sir James and Lady Ann were soon to meet, and the Duke of Gretton's pleasure was not to be permitted to come first. Nevertheless, perhaps it would be wise to take the precaution of requesting the chairmen to wait.

"Please wait here, for I may require you again," she said.

"Ma'am." Again they exchanged curious glances, for they recognized the duke's carriage. What was all this about, they wondered? Leaning back against the chair, they folded their arms and stared after her as she made her way toward the door of the house.

The coachman's jaw dropped as he noticed her, and he turned on his seat to watch in amazement as she went boldly up to the door and knocked loudly. What was this? A *lady* calling at this hour?

At first there was no response to the knock, but just as Deborah raised her hand again, the door suddenly opened and a butler looked out inquiringly. He blinked a little on seeing her. "Madam?"

"I wish to speak to the Duke of Gretton," she said.

His eyes widened. "I, er, beg your pardon?"

"I believe I spoke clearly enough. Please tell the duke that Mrs. Marchant has called and wishes to speak to him urgently."

At that moment Kate herself appeared at the head of the staircase at the far end of the hall. She was dressed in a frilly pink muslin wrap that outlined her curvaceous figure very clearly indeed, and her mane of chestnut curls was brushed loose about her shoulders. "What is it, Ladbury?" she inquired.

He cleared his throat uncomfortably and turned to look at the actress. "Madam, it's a Mrs. Marchant. She says she wishes to speak to the duke."

"Marchant?" The way Kate repeated the name conveyed that she knew who the caller was.

A second figure appeared at the top of the staircase. It was the duke. He ran his hand through his gray hair, looking down at Deborah in astonishment. Then his astonishment turned to irritated disbelief. "Mrs. Marchant?"

"I wish to speak to you, sir."

"Do you, indeed? Might I point out that by coming here you have broken many an unwritten rule?"

"The situation calls for it, sir."

"From which I take it that it concerns your brother?"

"My lord, you gave me your word that if I should discover anything which would prove Sir James to be lying, then you would hear me out. I have found something out which in my opinion it is imperative that you know of without further delay."

He came down the staircase, but Kate remained where she was. Her gaze hadn't left Deborah, whose face was revealed by the light of another candle mounted on the wall close to the door.

At the foot of the staircase, the duke halted. "Very well, Mrs. Marchant, since you are sufficiently convinced of the importance of what you have to say, I will listen to you."

Deborah stepped hesitantly into the entrance hall, lowering her hood as she did so. She was very conscious of Kate's intent gaze.

"What have you discovered, Mrs. Marchant?" the duke inquired, his blue eyes cool and unencouraging.

She glanced uneasily at Kate and at the butler, who still lingered by the door.

The duke drew a long breath. "Please tell me what you have come to say, madam," he said a little testily.

"Simply that in a short while Sir James Uppingham will call upon Lady Ann Appleby at her house, and that he will not arrive at the front door, but will go in from the mews lane."

He stared at her. "And how, pray, did you come by this astonishing information?"

"Lady Ann spoke to him in the Upper Rooms just after you and Lady Sabrina left."

"Mrs. Marchant, I am given to understand that Lady

Ann is unwell at the moment and that she did not attend the ball.''

"She was there, but only briefly. My lord, I would not have come here to see you unless I felt the matter was vital. From what I overheard them saying, it is clear that Lady Ann is being forced to do things she doesn't wish to do." Deborah briefly related the conversation she had overheard.

When she had finished, the duke was silent for a moment, and then he met her gaze. "Madam, if this is some invention on your part—"

"Do you honestly imagine I would come here like this simply to tell you a fabrication?" Deborah cried, sudden resentment bright in her eyes.

Kate descended the staircase. "Rowan, I think you should accept that what the lady says is true, for the actress in me recognizes full well when someone else is *not* acting. Mrs. Marchant really did overheard that conversation."

Deborah gave her a grateful look, but her glance was met with a cool response. The actress may have felt obliged to side briefly with her, but she was by no means a friend. With that cool response a gauntlet was flung down, and it was an invisible challenge of which Deborah was very conscious indeed.

The duke did not notice the silent exchange. "Very well, Mrs. Marchant, it seems I must take you seriously. I will go to Great Pulteney Street directly."

Deborah shook her head. "*We* will go to Great Pulteney Street," she corrected.

"I hardly think—"

"Sir, if your concern in all this is the protection of your sister, mine is the well-being of my brother. I refuse to stay away when something as vital as this is to take place.'' She was both defiant and determined. ''I prefer to have the evidence of my own ears and eyes, my lord, as I am sure you will understand.''

''From which I must presume that you do not trust me to faithfully relate what I see and hear,'' he replied caustically.

''I have no reason to trust you in this, sir, for you will put your sister's interests well before my brother's. You've made it clear that she must be saved from scandal at all costs, and from that I take it that you would consign my brother to ruin if necessary.''

''You do not know me at all, madam, and so I would thank you not to leap to conclusions. It so happens that I would put justice before either my sister or your brother, and I trust that in future you will remember that. We will go together, and your eyes and ears can do as they wish. Ladbury, my coat, if you please.''

''Your Grace.''

As his attention was momentarily diverted, Deborah felt obliged to apologize to Kate for having intruded, although she knew the apology would not be well received and could not blame the actress. ''Mrs. Hatherley, I am sorry to have imposed upon you like this.''

''Are you? I doubt that very much, Mrs. Marchant.'' Kate's hazel eyes flickered. ''We will speak again, madam, of that you may be sure.''

Nothing more was said, for the duke was ready to leave. ''Shall we go, Mrs. Marchant?''

''Sir.''

Inclining her head at Kate, Deborah raised her hood and went back out into the night. Within a moment or so her chairmen had been dismissed, and she and the duke were in his carriage en route for Great Pulteney Street.

Chapter 14

The hour was up when the carriage halted in one of the small culs-de-sac which led off Great Pulteney Street, and Deborah and the duke alighted to hurry across the street to the long flight of steps which lay alongside Lady Ann's house. Descending, they reached the low-lying mews lane behind. It was a dark, narrow way, linked with stables, coach houses, garden walls, and overhanging trees with very few lights to pierce the shadows. Sir James's carriage was already drawn up a little farther along from the wicket gate giving on to Lady Ann's garden, and of the coachman there was no sign.

One of the nearby coach house doors stood open, allowing lantern light and an occasional murmur of male voices to creep out into the night, and the duke left Deborah by the wicket gate for a moment as he went to look briefly inside. He saw a group of servants playing dice on the straw-strewn floor, and among them he recognized Sir James's coachman.

He returned to Deborah and glanced up toward the house. There was a light shining in a downstairs window, with a very inviting chink in the curtains. It was unlikely to be servants, for it was an above-stairs room, and the obvious possibility was that it was where Lady Ann and Sir James were facing each other.

The duke looked at Deborah, an inquiring eyebrow raised. "Shall we trespass, Mrs. Marchant?"

"I believe we must, sir, for I think we will be able to see through that crack in the curtains."

With a gloved hand he pushed the gate open and ushered her through, and then they began to make their way up a narrow gravel path toward the lighted window. There were several small flights of steps and a little terrace where a fountain would play in the summer. The water was still now, and as the moon came from behind a cloud, its light shone softly in the raised ornamental pool.

There was another terrace directly by the house, and below it the basement windows of the kitchens and other cellars. The servants hadn't retired to their beds yet and could be seen seated around a well-scrubbed table enjoying a cup of their mistress's best chocolate as they whiled away the minutes until they could go to sleep.

Suddenly the kitchen door opened, and light flooded out almost to where Deborah and the duke stood on the path. He swiftly pulled her back out of the sight among the shrubs, but the maid who came out didn't see anything amiss as she bent to pick up a wooden pail and then go back inside. She closed the door, and the light was extinguished again. On the terrace above the light continued to shine in the above-stairs window.

Deborah gazed up toward it, praying that Lady Ann and Sir James were indeed behind those curtains.

The duke stepped out from the shrubs and nodded toward some balustraded steps at the far end of the terrace. "Come on, if we are to see through that chink in the curtains, we must go up there."

She hesitated, and he held out his hand. Slowly she took it, and he led her past the kitchen door to the steps. Within moments they were on the terrace, tiptoeing toward the light.

By pressing close together, they could just see inside. It was a rather severe dining room, with dark green brocade on the walls and gilded niches in which stood white marble busts of Roman emperors. The long table was made of dark, highly polished mahogany, and there were twelve high-backed chairs ranged around it. Lady Ann sat on one of the chairs, her hands clasped restlessly on the table before her. Her face was ravaged by tears, and her long jet earrings trembled a little as she strove to maintain what little composure she had left. She still wore the mauve evening gown, and there was something heartrendingly affecting about the way she closed her eyes and swallowed from time to time.

At first there was no sign of Sir James, but then he stepped into view on the other side of the table from Lady Ann. His face was hard and cold as he leaned his hands upon the polished mahogany and spoke to her. It was impossible to hear what he said, but he gestured toward a portrait on the wall at the end of the room, and with an audible cry Lady Ann hid her face in her hands.

Both Deborah and the duke looked at the portrait. It was of a young girl of about fourteen, dressed in a white muslin gown with a wide blue sash around her high waist. She was a pretty girl, and very like Lady Ann, with the same olive skin, dark brown eyes, and lustrous dark brown hair, and at first Deborah took it to be a portrait of Lady Ann herself as a child, but then she realized that the portrait was too recent in style for that. Whoever the girl was, she wasn't Lady Ann Appleby. Sir James's threat at the Upper Rooms sounded in her head. *I also suggest that you would do well to bear Chippenham in mind.*

Suddenly Sir James's fist crashed down upon the table, and Lady Ann flinched, staring up into his snarling face. He pointed again at the portrait, and Lady Ann began to nod. His fist thundered on the mahogany again, and Lady Ann rose trembling to her feet, her voice suddenly so shrill with dread that her words carried clearly out into the night.

"Yes, yes, I will do whatever you say, only please don't harm Christabel. I will stay in Bath, I will hold firm to our story about poor Mr. Wexford, and not a word of the truth will pass my lips!"

Sir James straightened, a satisfied smile upon his full lips. He spoke again, but his soft tones could not be heard. Then he turned on his heel and left the room. Behind him Lady Ann dissolved into tears.

Deborah drew back, turning to look challengingly at the duke. "*Now* do you believe me that Sir James isn't the paragon he pretends to be?"

"Mrs. Marchant, I believe every word you say, but if we stay here a moment longer, we run the risk of being caught!" he breathed, snatching her hand and almost dragging her away from the window toward the steps.

They ran down toward the garden and were on the gravel path when the door of the house opened behind them, and Sir James emerged. He paused for a moment, his tall lean figure silhouetted against the lamplight within, and then he tapped on his tall hat and began to descend the same path toward the mews lane and his waiting carriage.

Deborah's heart was pounding as she and the duke reached the wicket gate. If they went through, surely they would be seen by the light from the coach house opposite, where the game of dice was still in progress.

"Keep your head, low, Mrs. Marchant," instructed the duke, opening the gate and thrusting her through.

Bending almost double in her efforts not to be seen, she stumbled out into the shadowy lane and then turned toward the steps on the corner. The duke followed, but as they began to go up, they saw a figure descending slowly toward them. It was Sir James's coachman.

With a curse, the duke tugged his tall hat down further over his hair, and caught Deborah's arm. Before she knew what was happening he had thrust her against the wall of Lady Ann's house, his other arm tight around her waist. His whisper was low and urgent. "The fellow knows me, Mrs. Marchant, and if we go back the way we've come we'll almost certainly encounter Uppingham. I don't want him to know just yet that the game is up, and so I suggest a little subterfuge."

"Subterfuge?"

"The coachman will walk past without a second thought if he sees a gentleman dallying with a lady of questionable virtue."

Deborah's eyes widened. "What exactly do you expect me to do?" she breathed, a multitude of startling possibilities running through her mind.

"Just behave with a little abandon," he murmured, and before she could say anything more he pressed closer, his lips over hers.

The past few seconds had caught her so off guard

that she couldn't move. She closed her eyes, conscious even at such a desperate moment as this that it felt inordinately good to be kissed by him.

He drew back fleetingly, his lips close to her ear. "Madam, a *belle de nuit* would behave more wantonly."

Suddenly she was mistress of her wits again, and she linked her arms around his neck. "I will be as wanton as you wish, my lord," she whispered, reaching up to kiss him.

A thousand and one conflicting emotions washed through her as she gave herself to the embrace. Memories of how she'd loathed him vied with the knowledge that his smiles had reached effortlessly past her anger. This man had stirred the heart that had lain dormant for so long, and the warmth of his lips began to arouse a desire that paid no heed to the hazardous situation she was in. At any moment the coachman might recognize the duke, even though his tall hat was pulled low over his unmistakable hair, and Sir James himself might come to the corner and see them both, but in spite of this she surrendered to the intense pleasure now holding complete sway over her senses. She almost wished she were a woman of easy virtue, who wouldn't give a second thought to submitting out here in the darkness of the night. She was ashamed of her thoughts but could not deny their existence. She desired the Duke of Gretton, she wanted to be taken by him, made complete love to by him, and held in his arms like this forever. There was no modesty or virtue in such thoughts, no modesty or virtue at all.

The coachman had almost reached them now, and the duke hid his face from all chance of detection by bending his head to kiss her throat. Her breath escaped on an audible sigh as his lips moved softly against her pulse, and she held him close, her whole body alive and responsive.

The coachman was whistling to himself, and the whistle broke off briefly as he heard her sigh. A knowing grin broke out on his lips as he glanced at the lucky swell with the willing whore. He didn't know he was looking at the Duke of Gretton, nor did he know that the whore was a fashionable lady, for all he could see of Deborah was her purple cloak, dulled to anonymous black in the darkness. Resuming his whistling, he strolled on past and disappeared around the corner, where he was immediately confronted by an extremely irritated Sir James, who demanded to know where he'd been.

Their raised voices were only a few feet away and Deborah drew away uneasily, her anxious gaze turned toward the corner, but the duke put his hand to her chin. "Not yet, Mrs. Marchant, not yet," he murmured, kissing her again.

His lips moved skillfully over hers, and Sir James Uppingham faded from her thoughts as once more she was distracted by the beguiling sensuality of his embrace.

It wasn't until they both heard the sound of Sir James's carriage driving away along the mews lane that the duke relaxed his hold, although he didn't release her completely. He looked down into her eyes. "Your talent for such subterfuge is nothing short of breathtaking, Mrs. Marchant," he observed softly.

She was glad of the darkness, for it hid the embarrassed color staining her hot cheeks. "You requested a little abandon, my lord," she pointed out, hoping that he did not detect the utter turmoil she was in.

"A little abandon, yes, but I did not expect such wholehearted enthusiasm."

She was mortified. "If I went too far, then I must ask you to forgive me."

"Oh, please don't misunderstand, for I'm not complaining. Far from it, in fact." He gave the faintest of smiles, and then released her. Removing his hat, he ran his fingers through his hair, and then glanced toward Lady Ann's house. "To the matter in hand, Mrs. Marchant. I now fully accept that Uppingham isn't the fine fellow he claims to be, indeed what I've witnessed tonight makes me view him with utter contempt. No gentleman should ever treat a lady as he treated Lady Ann, and I have no intention whatsoever of allowing him to remain betrothed to my sister. What I cannot understand, though, is why he has done all this. Why go to such lengths to incriminate your brother? What purpose lies behind it all?"

Deborah couldn't meet his eyes.

He put a quick hand to her chin and forced her to look at him. "There's something you aren't telling me, isn't there?"

"I don't want to say anything more, not just yet, my lord."

"Dammit, woman, you can't get me to this point and then suddenly become coy! You were the one who insisted that I come here tonight, and now I expect you to tell me everything!"

"It isn't for me to tell you, my lord. I must first speak to . . ." Her voice died away.

He searched her face in the darkness. "There's only one person you seem to have been trying to speak to, Mrs. Marchant, and that is my sister. Has this something to do with Sabrina?"

Deborah nodded unwillingly.

"Remain silent, by all means, but I will keep you here until you tell me, you may be sure of that," he declared, folding his arms and waiting.

She drew a long breath, and then gave in. "Very well, my lord, I will tell you everything I know." She told him about Richard's letter and the pocket watch, and everything else, right up to her success in at last extracting a promise from Sabrina to meet her the next day at the Milsom Street dressmaker.

When she had finished, he was silent for a long moment, and then he looked at her. "Your brother and my sister intended to elope?"

"Yes, and they would have done had not Sir James found out about them and gone to all these lengths to make Richard appear the villain. At least, that is what I think happened. I don't think Lady Sabrina knows he discovered her secret. Sir James loves her, and finding out that she was in love with my brother would, in my opinion, give him all the reason he needed to concoct this story of stolen necklaces and seduction. If you do not believe me about the planned elopement, at least the inscription on the watch proves that she was very much in love with Richard."

"There is no need to prove anything further, Mrs. Marchant, for I believe you. I only wish that Sabrina had trusted me enough to confide in me herself."

"I think she was ashamed of having allowed things to go so far, my lord. She knew that you and Sir James were proceeding with arrangements for the betrothal, and she still went on letting that happen even though she knew it was my brother she really loved."

"Richard Wexford isn't entirely without blame in all

this, Mrs. Marchant. He should have come to me and been open about it.''

Deborah nodded. ''I do not deny it, sir, but in all fairness I have to say that it would be very difficult indeed to tell you the truth when it was clear that you wished above all else to carry out your late father's wishes.''

''Difficult, but not impossible.''

''Perhaps Lady Sabrina preferred an elopement, which would at least have given her the protection of my brother's name. To be open about it all before the event would have exposed her to scandal, and I think that that is the one thing she fears above all else. She was terrified when my identity was revealed in the conservatory, for she thought her secret was about to be dragged into the open.''

He nodded. ''You are probably right.''

''I think, too, that her recent illness has been caused by her belief that Richard not only stole the necklace, but also that he was conducting a liaison with Lady Ann. Your sister is suffering from a broken heart, my lord.''

''Broken hearts are the stuff of novels, Mrs. Marchant.''

''But they do exist, I promise you.''

He smiled at her. ''Yes, I suppose they do,'' he murmured.

She returned the smile. ''I'm glad now that I've told you everything,'' she said.

''Contrary to your belief, madam, I am not an ogre, even though I may have appeared to have gone out of my way to give that impression of late. I love my sister very much, and her happiness means a great deal to me. If Richard Wexford is the man she really loves, then she will have my blessing to follow her heart, make no mistake of that. But first we must prove once and for all that he is innocent, and Uppingham is guilty.'' He glanced at Lady Ann's house again. "I rather fancy that our cause will be best served by an immediate call upon that unfortunate lady. I have a feeling that she will help us if I can convince her that I can protect her from Uppingham.''

"If she is being blackmailed through whoever that girl is in the portrait, I cannot see that anything you say will persuade her to assist us.''

"Uppingham isn't the only one capable of issuing threats, Mrs. Marchant, for I can stir myself to considerable unpleasantness when the spirit moves me. You may or may not be aware that I am regarded as one of the most accurate shots in England, and I am quite prepared to call him out. He would not emerge the victor from such a dawn meeting, I assure you.''

She stared at him. "A duel?'' she breathed.

"If necessary, but I do not for a moment imagine it will come to that. I believe that Uppingham can be persuaded to do as we wish rather than run the risk of being extinguished at my hand. With a little cunning on our part, I think we can achieve not only your brother's exoneration from all blame, but also Lady Ann's protection from blackmail, and the continuing concealment of my sister's, er, secret misconduct.''

Deborah searched his face in the darkness. "Do you really believe we can achieve all that?''

"Yes, Mrs. Marchant, I do.'' He paused for a moment. "Forgive me for saying this, but are you absolutely confident that there has never been anything between Lady Ann and your brother? I do not pretend to know Richard at all, indeed we've only spoken on a few occasions, but it isn't beyond the realms of possibility that he finds older women to his liking. Lady Ann is a very handsome woman, after all.''

"If Richard was guilty in that respect, he would not have written a denial in his letter to me. In the letter he told of his undying love for Lady Sabrina, and he refuted entirely all suggestion of a liaison with Lady Ann.''

"And you believe him completely?''

"Yes.''

"Then that is sufficient for me.''

"My lord, you hardly know me. I may be the most dreadful judge of character.''

He gave a low laugh. "My dear Mrs. Marchant, after what passed between us a few minutes ago, I feel I know you exceptionally well.''

The darkness again hid her embarrassment. "My lord, after what passed between us a few minutes ago, you know only that I have a talent for subterfuge.''

"Ah, yes. Subterfuge,'' he murmured dryly, putting on his hat. "Well, whatever your talent is, Mrs. Marchant, I can vouch for its effects. I don't know when I was last taken quite so much by surprise. I confess to more than a little disappointment that the coachman walked straight past, for who knows to what delights I might have been treated had he lingered awhile.''

"You would probably have been deeply disappointed, my lord,'' she replied, trying to appear composed when she was not.

"We will never know now, will we?'' he said. "Now then, shall we call upon Lady Ann?'' Offering her his arm, he indicated that they should climb the steps and go to the front of the house. As he did so however, they both heard the sound of running footsteps on the gravel path in the garden, and a moment later a man's voice rang out urgently to the grooms and stableboys still playing dice in the coach house.

"Let's be having you, my lads! Lady Ann's leaving for Chippenham without delay and needs her traveling carriage right now! Get a move on, for she's in a great hurry!"

Chapter 15

The duke's loud knocking brought Lady Ann's harassed butler at the double, but as he opened the door he was startled and dismayed to find himself brushed aside as the duke and Deborah entered the house uninvited. They found themselves in an entrance hall where chaos reigned as Lady Ann's hasty preparations to leave had all the servants hurrying about in confusion. A footman was dragging a hastily packed trunk down the stairs, and two maids ran up past him with garments that had been freshly laundered that day.

After his initial shock at being treated so unceremoniously, the butler recovered his dignity. "May I inquire the meaning of this, sir, madam?" he enquired.

The duke tossed his hat and gloves down upon a table and turned to face him. "Please inform Lady Ann that the Duke of Gretton wishes to speak to her immediately."

The butler gaped. The Duke of Gretton? "Your . . . Your Grace, I fear that Lady Ann cannot possibly receive visitors now, for not only is it exceedingly late, but she is also about to depart for Chippenham."

"Tell her that what I have to say to her is to her advantage. We will wait in there." Indicating the dining room, the duke turned and walked away, as if Lady Ann's acquiescence was a foregone conclusion. As Deborah followed him, the bothered butler decided to do as he was told, for it wasn't up to him to argue with dukes. With a resigned sigh he went up the stairs to tell his mistress.

In the dining room, which was now lit only by several candlesticks on the mantelshelf, Deborah and the duke went to study the portrait that Sir James had used earlier to force Lady Ann to obey him. The girl's painted face gazed sweetly down at them from the canvas, her dark brown eyes so lifelike that it seemed she might at any moment step down from the frame.

Deborah glanced at the duke. "Who do you think she is?"

"Well, we know that her name is Christabel," he murmured, "and if my guess is correct, I believe we will find that she is Lady Ann's daughter."

Deborah's lips parted in surprise. "Her daughter? But Lady Ann has never married."

"My dear Mrs. Marchant, since when has conception been dependent upon the presence of a marriage contract?"

"Since never, sir, but I confess to being a little skeptical of the suggestion that someone like Lady Ann would have a child out of wedlock."

"But if she had, would it not be an excellent lever for a blackmailer?" he murmured. "Look at the portrait, Mrs. Marchant, how can it be a likeness of anyone other than Lady Ann's child? The hair is the same, the eyes and the complexion match exactly, and yet the painting cannot be more than three or four years old at the most. I would lay odds that Christabel can call Lady Ann Appleby her mother."

The door opened behind them, and Lady Ann herself came hesitantly in. She still looked quite distraught, although she had conquered her tears. Her eyes were tear-stained and puffy, and her straight black hair had been combed loose and then tied back with a simple green silk ribbon. She now wore a plain green velvet gown.

"You wished to see me urgently, Your Grace?" she said to the duke, but then froze as she recognized Deborah, to whose real identity she had evidently now been alerted. With a faint gasp she backed away toward the door again, but in a moment the duke strode over to her and took her hand.

"Please don't be afraid, Lady Ann, for we mean you no malice or harm, on the contrary in fact."

"I . . . I have nothing to say . . ."

"We know that Uppingham is blackmailing you, Lady Ann, and we know that you have been compelled to tell lies about Mrs. Marchant's brother, Richard Wexford. If you will but trust yourself to me, I think I can promise that we can defeat Uppingham, and that all will end well."

Her lips trembled, and her hand crept anxiously to the lace at her throat as her eyes went from him to Deborah. "I'm afraid to say anything to you, sir," she whispered. "I *dare* not say anything . . ."

"Because he has threatened your daughter?"

Lady Ann's breath caught, and she snatched her hand away. "I don't have a daughter!" she cried.

"Yes, you do, my lady, for that is her portrait," said the duke, pointing.

Tears filled her eyes, and she shook her head. "No. No, she's isn't my daughter . . ."

Deborah went to her, taking her hand and drawing

her toward one of the chairs by the table. "Please sit down, Lady Ann, for the duke and I mean to stop Sir James from succeeding in any of this. Maybe we are wrong, and Christabel isn't your daughter, but whoever she is, she is important enough for you to be vulnerable because of her."

Lady Ann sat down unwillingly, her tearful gaze moving toward the portrait. Deborah sat next to her, and the duke leaned back against the heavy table, but when he again asked her to confide in them, she still shook her head. "I have nothing to say to you."

He was gently persuasive. "Lady Ann, I will protect you from Uppingham, you have my word upon that. You don't have to fear him."

"I don't fear him for myself, not anymore, but I do fear him because of Christabel. You are right, she is my daughter." She hesitated, staring at the portrait, and then she sighed resignedly. "I will tell you what you want to know, for I suppose it makes no difference now. My mind is made up, and I know what I must do. It began three weeks ago, when Sir James suddenly called upon me very late one night. He and I weren't acquainted at all, and naturally I was puzzled to say the least, but it soon became clear that the call was not one of friendship. He told me that he had found out about Christabel, and that he would make me the subject of a public scandal unless I did what he wanted. You see, he incorrectly believed she'd been born out of wedlock, but nevertheless I have always been terrified that her existence would become known."

Deborah looked curiously at her. "I don't understand. If Christabel is legitimate, why are you. . . ?"

"It is a long story, Mrs. Marchant, and begins sixteen years ago when I was only sixteen myself. A small estate adjoining my father's land in Hertfordshire was sold to a gentleman named George Arrowsmith, and from the first moment I saw him, I loved him with all my heart. He wasn't considered suitable however, for not only was he far below me in station, but he was also involved in a boundary dispute with my father over the ownership of some prime land that had been in the Appleby family for several centuries. My father loathed George, especially when against all the odds he won the dispute and my father had to part with the land. Fearful of losing me to George as well, my father despatched me to distant relatives in Scotland, but George followed me.'' Lady Ann's eyes shimmered with tears. ''We were married without anyone knowing, but we spent only one night together, for when he left me the next morning his horse bolted and threw him, and he was killed when his head struck a rock. I was inconsolable and frightened because I was suddenly alone. No one knew of my secret marriage, and I took refuge in keeping it a secret, for without George I lacked all courage. Then I discovered I was expecting his child, and I was forced to confide in one of my relatives. She agreed to help me, but only provided I gave up my child afterward, and no one was ever any the wiser. I agreed to her terms, and in due course I had Christabel. I couldn't bring myself to give her up entirely however, and so I made certain she was cared for properly, and I provided for her as best I could from my allowance. I saw her as often as I could, and she and I are now very close. My father never knew what had happened, and as the years have passed it has become more and more difficult to tell him. He never forgave George for succeeding in the law suit or for being upstart enough to attempt to court me, and when he learned of George's sudden death from a riding accident, he expressed satisfaction that he was now rid of such an unwelcome neighbor. I am deeply ashamed of my weakness in shrinking from the facts of what I'd done, but in spite of everything I still love my father very much. He is very old and frail now, and the shock of discovering how greatly I deceived and disappointed him would probably put an end to him. I couldn't bear to have that on my conscience as well, and so I've continued to keep Christabel's existence a deep secret. That is why I was originally so vulnerable to blackmail. Now I am fearful too that Sir James is prepared to harm Christabel should I defy him.'' Lady Ann bowed her head, her shoulders shaking as she began to cry.

Deborah put out a comforting hand. ''Please don't cry, Lady Ann, for I understand your quandary.''

''Do you?'' Lady Ann took a deep steadying breath. ''I am so ashamed of my actions, both in the past and again now. I denied my love for George, denied my marriage, and, above all, denied the existence of my beloved child. Now I have been craven enough to submit to a plot to dishonor and ruin your poor brother.'' She rose unhappily to her feet. ''Sir James made no secret of his reasons for doing it. He was in love with Lady Sabrina and found out that she was secretly seeing Mr. Wexford. He intended to rid himself of such a formidable rival by incriminating him, and by allowing Lady Sabrina to also believe that a liaison of some sort had taken place. He wanted it to appear that Mr. Wexford had seduced me in order to steal the necklace, and to my regret I agreed. Sir James also wanted us to pretend that we were still not acquainted because he felt it would strengthen our plot, for no one would imagine we had conspired together if it was believed we didn't know each other. The whispers about my indiscretions with Mr. Wexford were hard to tolerate, but I was prepared to do anything to protect the secret about my daughter.''

The duke studied her. "What happened to make you change your mind? Why did you suddenly go to the ball tonight and risk so much by doing so?''

She turned swiftly. "How did you know I went there? I was only at the rooms for a few minutes. I saw you and Lady Sabrina leaving, and then I managed to speak briefly to Sir James.''

Deborah looked at her. "I was there as well, Lady Ann. I was hiding behind the curtain right next to you because I didn't want to be seen by the duke, Lady Sabrina, or Sir James. I had to stay there when Sir James saw you, and I overheard everything you said. It was because of what I heard that I went to see the duke, and then we came here. We, er, were also eavesdropping a little earlier, when Sir James was in this room with you. We were outside the window.'' She nodded toward the drawn curtains.

Lady Ann gave a brief, rather ironic laugh. "I had no idea, no idea at all,'' she murmured, then she took a long breath. "You asked why I suddenly changed my mind. I will tell you. When Sir James learned today that you were Mr. Wexford's sister, Mrs. Marchant, he immediately sent a message to me so that I would be on my guard. But discovering who you were, and knowing that you'd come anonymously with Morag McNeil, who must have known your real identity, unnerved me completely. I knew that you and Morag must have had an ulterior motive for calling here, and that that could only mean you suspected me. I was afraid that I was about to be exposed, and since I already felt wretched with guilt, I suddenly couldn't stand it anymore. I decided that I would leave Bath without further ado, go to Christabel, whose whereabouts I didn't then realize were known to Sir James, and then take her somewhere secret and safe. Once I had come to that decision, nothing would do but that I faced Sir James immediately. I didn't care that I ran a great risk by going to the Upper Rooms, for I was wound up to such a point that I really wasn't thinking clearly. I had one thing in my mind, one thing only, and that was to run away with my daughter. But, as you know, Mrs. Marchant, when I told him what I'd decided to do, he made it clear that he knew exactly where to find my daughter. Somehow he had found out that she is in Chippenham. For the past year she has been at Miss Algernon's Academy for the Daughters of Gentlefolk, and she is there under her real name, Christabel Arrowsmith.''

Deborah's lips parted, and she remembered the wrought iron gates and cedar-lined drive leading to the redbrick mansion on the outskirts of the Wiltshire market town. She had driven right past the place where Sir James Uppingham's weapon of blackmail was to be found!

Lady Ann continued. ''If you were outside the window a little earlier, you know what transpired when Sir James came here. I gave in again when he threatened to go to Chippenham, but when he had gone I decided that my only course was to run away before he knew it, and take Christabel with me. I knew that would mean the inevitable spread of my daughter's story, my illegitimate daughter as he believed, and that it would reach my father, but the time has come for me to put Christabel before all else. My father is old and has had a long and full life; Christabel's life is just beginning. I wish I could help you in whatever it is you have planned, but I am set upon going to Chippenham to take my daughter away. She is going to be safe from him, and that is all that matters to me.''

As if to emphasize the finality of her words, her carriage was at that moment brought to the door. The stamping and snorting of the fresh horses became suddenly louder as the butler opened the front door for the first of the trunks to be carried out.

The duke went to the window and held the curtain aside to look out at the night. Beyond the river the lights of Bath twinkled in the darkness. Lowering the curtain once more, he turned back to face Lady Ann. "I have a suggestion to make, Lady Ann, but first I need to know whether you would still decline to help if you knew beyond all shadow of doubt that Christabel was safe.''

"Safe?''

"Beyond Uppingham's reach at some unknown address. Lady Ann, you do not have to be the one to remove your daughter from the school, for Mrs. Marchant and I could go in your stead, provided, of course, that you gave us the necessary letter of authority to give to her headmistress. We could leave for Chippenham tonight, be there by breakfast time, and have your daughter safely back here in Bath before noon, while Uppingham and my sister are at the military display on Claverton Down.''

Lady Ann drew back, shaking her head. "Bring her here? Oh, no, I cannot agree to that, for it is too close to him, and if he should find out—''

"I don't mean this house in particular, Lady Ann, but rather was I thinking of the house on Royal Crescent where Mrs. Marchant is staying with Mrs. McNeil."

Deborah was already astonished to have been nominated to go to Chippenham with him, and she was even more so when she heard him mention his choice of hiding place for Christabel.

His attention was still upon Lady Ann. "It could be accomplished with ease, and Uppingham would be none the wiser, especially if you were still here, apparently complying with his orders. He is taking my sister to the military display on Claverton Down tomorrow morning, but on her return, we can all band together to discuss what we must do to defeat him. What do you say, Lady Ann? Surely it is better to make a stand with friends and allies, than to submit to Uppingham, or to risk fleeing for somewhere unknown?"

She hesitated. "How do I know that I can really trust you?" she asked at last.

"Because we both have as much reason as you to want Uppingham punished. I want my sister to be free of him, and I want him to pay a suitable price for his villainy. Mrs. Marchant wishes her brother's name to be cleared."

Lady Ann lowered her gaze to the floor and was silent for a long moment, but when she looked up again, there was a sense of new purpose about her. "Very well, Your Grace, I will help you."

A rush of relief passed over Deborah, for surely with the desertion of his only ally, Sir James would soon be vanquished.

The duke crossed the room to take Lady Ann's

149

hands. "You will not regret your decision, I promise you. Now, you must dismiss your carriage, and then write the necessary letter for us to take to the school."

"I will do both things immediately," she replied, and hurried from the room.

The duke then turned to Deborah. "Mrs. Marchant, I trust you do not mind being dragooned into the role of Christabel's chaperone?"

"Mind? Of course not."

"I trust also that that reassurance extends to my rather high-handed choice of hiding place?"

"Well, I certainly do not mind, sir, and I am equally certain that Mrs. McNeil will not have any objection, for she is anxious to prove that Richard did not do any of the things of which he stands accused. She is as keen as I to see Sir James in court."

He paused. "That may not be entirely practical," he said after a moment.

She looked quickly at him. "Why do you say that?"

"Because we must do what we can to protect the reputations of both Lady Ann and my sister, and Uppingham will be as detrimental as he can if he appears in court. Can you imagine the things he might choose to say of them? I intend to deny him that opportunity and think that instead of seeing that he is arrested, it would be better simply to extract a written confession from him in which he admits to having stolen the necklace himself in order to incriminate your brother, toward whom he bears a grudge. I will then advise him that he will be given time to leave the country in order to avoid arrest, but he will be warned that if he spreads any whispers at all about the ladies concerned, then he will have me to answer to. It will not be an idle threat on my part, as he will know full well, and I rather think he will hold his tongue."

Deborah nodded. "I know I would," she murmured.

He smiled. "Mrs. Marchant, I have every reason to be grateful to you."

"To me? Why?"

"If it had not been for your fierce determination to clear your brother's name no matter what, all this might not have come to light, and Sabrina would have been bound to him forever. I am dismayed to realize that I was so blind to him, and to Sabrina's unhappiness."

"You must not reproach yourself, for it wasn't your fault, and the moment you knew the truth, you acted. Nothing more could be asked of you."

He smiled again. "You have a way with you, madam; indeed I fancy you could persuade Old Nick himself that he isn't so bad a fellow after all."

Taking her hand, he drew it palm uppermost to his lips.

Chapter 16

It was still dark as Deborah stepped out of the primrose satin gown, and Amy helped her to put on a much warmer leaf green dress and matching pelisse for the journey to Chippenham. The clock on the mantelpiece stood at half-past five as she then went to sit at the dressing table for the maid to dress her hair a little more simply than the coiffure required for the ball.

Mrs. McNeil sat by the fire, having been aroused from her bed to hear what had transpired during the night. Without its customary powder her hair was salt and pepper in color, and hung in long plaits from beneath her muslin night bonnet. She wore a comfortable peach velvet wrap over her nightgown, and her feet were stretched out toward the warmth of the fire, for she was fortunate enough not to suffer from the agonies of chilblains.

She had been astonished and delighted at the turn events had taken and was glad to learn that Lady Ann had not been Sir James's willing accomplice. She was of the sincere hope that Richard Wexford's fortunes were about to change, but her eyes bore a rather troubled expression as she watched Deborah. There was a glow about her the older woman thought, and it was a glow that was only partly due to the imminent prospect of defeating Sir James Uppingham. If Mrs. McNeil was not mistaken, the rest of that telltale glow was due to the Duke of Gretton, with whom Deborah would shortly be entirely alone during the journey to Chippenham. It was all quite proper, of course, for widows were permitted a great deal of latitude, and such things as chaperones were not mandatory, but nevertheless Mrs. McNeil was worried. She had already become concerned about the change in Deborah's attitude toward the duke, but now the change had become so marked as to make the older woman anxious on her behalf. To look at Deborah Marchant now was to look at a woman who had begun to live again after three years of loneliness; but how did the duke feel? Everyone knew that he was passionately involved with Kate Hatherley; indeed Deborah had found him at the actress's house that very night, so it was very unlikely indeed that he shared the emotion now shining in Deborah's lovely gray eyes. If Rowan Sinclair had given cause for such feelings to stir, then in Mrs. McNeil's opinion he had either done so unwittingly, or as a passing amusement, but certainly not because Deborah had supplanted Kate in his affections.

Becoming conscious of the other woman's thoughtful gaze, Deborah turned her head. "What is it, Mrs. McNeil? Do you have reservations about Christabel being brought here?"

"No, my dear, but I do have reservations about you traveling to Chippenham alone with the duke."

"But it's hardly improper," Deborah protested in some surprise.

"It isn't a question of propriety, my dear, but rather

one of wisdom. Deborah, are you quite sure it is sensible for you to accompany him like this?''

''Christabel must have a chaperone.''

''Yes, but I wish it was not to be you,'' Mrs. McNeil replied quietly.

''Why?''

''I think you know full well why, my dear.''

Deborah looked quickly away, unable to meet the shrewd sympathy in the other's eyes. She didn't want to admit to the way her feelings were taking her, nor did she wish to contemplate the inevitable painful ending.

Amy brought Deborah's leaf green silk hat, and Mrs. McNeil gave a silent sigh as the room became quiet once more. There was unhappiness in store, and all she could hope was that she would be there to give what comfort she could when it was needed.

There was a tap at the door, and Amy hurried to answer it. Sanders stood there. ''His Grace is waiting,'' he said.

Deborah rose in surprise, for she hadn't heard the carriage. ''The duke is here?'' she said.

''Yes, madam. You will not have heard anything because the carriage is in the mews lane, and His Grace came to the kitchen door. He felt it would be more discreet to do that than to risk being seen calling at such a very odd hour.''

Amy hastened to bring her mistress's reticule and gloves, and a few moments later Deborah was ready to leave.

Mrs. McNeil rose from her chair. ''Take care, my dear, for when this is over—''

Deborah interrupted quickly. ''Please don't say it, Mrs. McNeil, for I am only too conscious of the dangers,'' she said, before hurrying from the room to the head of the staircase, where the butler was waiting to conduct her down to the kitchen.

Mrs. McNeil gazed sadly after her. Fate was determined to be as cruel as possible to Deborah Marchant, first of all robbing her of the husband she'd adored, and now thrusting her headlong into a new emotional entanglement that was certain to come to nothing.

The duke was waiting in the deserted kitchen, where the only light was the glowing fire in the immense hearth. Flames danced above the fresh log that had been recently placed there, and the light flickered on the gleaming array of copper pots and pans hung against the walls. He wore his greatcoat and stood with one boot resting upon an andiron as he gazed down at the fire. His tall hat and gloves lay on the scrubbed oak table behind him, and the air was heavy with the smell of bread, which had been baked that evening in readiness for breakfast.

Sanders announced her and then withdrew, and the duke immediately straightened and turned toward her. His glance raked her from head to toe before coming to meet her eyes. ''Mrs. Marchant,'' he murmured, inclining his head briefly.

She felt rather self-conscious. ''It doesn't seem right that a duke should be kept waiting in a kitchen,'' she said.

He smiled. ''What's this, a belated respect for my rank? I seem to recall a healthy *dis*respect when first we met.''

''I would prefer to forget our first meeting, sir,'' she replied.

''It was a singular experience for me, I assure you, and it certainly reminded me that I am a mere mortal after all." He took something from his pocket. "Your property, I believe," he said, holding out her locket.

She took it, but as he saw that she intended to wear it, he quickly made to help her. "Allow me," he said, stepping behind her and placing the locket around her neck. She bent her head forward, closing her eyes as his fingers brushed the warm skin at the nape of her neck.

When he had finished, he went to the table to pick up his hat and gloves. "I trust Mrs. McNeil is well pleased with the progress we've made?"

"Yes."

The brevity of the answer could not be mistaken, and his blue eyes swung shrewdly toward her. "Is something wrong?"

"No, of course not," she replied, making her tone much more convincing. "What did Lady Sabrina say when you told her?"

"I haven't told her anything, indeed I haven't even disturbed her sleep."

Deborah stared at him. "Why not?"

"Because she is to spend this coming morning with Uppingham, and I don't know whether she is up to such a prolonged period of pretense. She hasn't been strong recently, as you know, and in my opinion it is wiser not to subject her to such an ordeal. I will tell her when she returns from Claverton Down." He hesitated. "I trust I've made the right decision, for I fear I've had cause to doubt my judgment of late."

"There is nothing wrong with your judgment, sir."

"You are far too kind," he replied dryly, tapping on his hat and then donning his gloves before offering her his arm. "I think we should leave without further delay, for although it is only thirteen miles to Chippenham, they are thirteen hilly miles and may take all of two hours to cover.''

She accepted the arm, and together they left the kitchen. Outside it was still very dark, but on the eastern horizon there was now the faintest hint of gray. Dawn wasn't far away now.

It was almost eight o'clock, and the sun had long since risen when Chippenham at last appeared ahead, but Deborah was unaware that they were almost at journey's end. The rhythm of the carriage was so lulling that in spite of her efforts to remain awake, she had at last succumbed to sleep. She knew nothing as the vehicle jolted over a rut in the road, or when the duke left his seat opposite to sit beside her with his arm around her shoulder.

In her dream she was far away from the Duke of Gretton, and the motion of the carriage had become the swaying of the rowing boat as Jonathan had rowed her out across the cove at St. Mary Magna. He hadn't been in his uniform, but wore only his shirt, waistcoat, and breeches, and his chestnut hair was shining in the heat of the August sun. His green eyes were warm and caressing as he glanced at her as she sat on the cushions in the stern of the boat. She wore a yellow-and-white gingham gown, her dark hair was tied loosely back with a white gauze scarf. A frilled white silk parasol twirled above her head.

The sea was still and blue, and the cove where later the *Thetis* was to founder was as gentle and calm as a mill pond. The gulls were quiet in the summer heat, so that the soaring song of the skylarks could be heard far above the nearby cliffs. It was a perfect day, and she and Jonathan were so much in love. So very much in love. And yet . . . She was conscious of a pang of guilt, for in her thoughts she had been unfaithful to him. Another man's smiles had distracted her, invading her thoughts so much that sometimes *his* name was first upon her lips, not Jonathan's.

As the shadow of conscience darkened her eyes, so the skies darkened overhead. The sun was obliterated by storm clouds and from nowhere the wind came to whip the seas into a fury. Waves crashed against the rocks, and the tiny boat was tossed about like a cork. She was too terrified to even scream, and could only stare in dismay as the sea swept Jonathan away, dragging him down into its depths and leaving no trace at all.

At last she found her tongue. "No!" she screamed. "No!"

"Mrs. Marchant?" The duke's concerned voice broke quietly into the nightmare.

For a moment the storm still had her in its grip, but then suddenly there was silence. Her eyes flew open on a stifled gasp, and she reached out instinctively to clutch his arm.

"It's all right, you're quite safe," he murmured reassuringly.

She stared at him. "I . . . I was dreaming."

"A nightmare, I fancy."

She still stared at him, for the dream's effect was strong and clear, as was its meaning. She did feel guilty, but not because she'd almost betrayed Jonathan's love in the past. It was now that she was betraying him, because the Duke of Gretton had stolen her heart. She loved this man, she loved him so much that there was nothing she could do to save herself.

The duke removed his glove and put his hand concernedly to her pale cheek. "What were you dreaming?"

Her breath caught, and she pulled swiftly away from him. "I . . . I don't remember."

He said nothing more, and a few minutes later the carriage slowed to turn in through the gates of Miss Algernon's Academy for the Daughters of Gentlefolk. As the coachman brought the team up to a smart trot along the cedar-lined drive toward the redbrick mansion, Deborah tried to regain her lost composure. Her fingers crept to enclose the locket. It was an instinctive action which the duke observed.

Miss Algernon was surprised and a little displeased to be brought from the comfort of her bed and morning tea. She was an elderly but surprisingly sprightly lady from Dublin, and she had no truck at all with those who did not observe the academy's rules. Visitors were very firmly requested to call during the afternoons and evenings, certainly not while the housemaids were about their business!

Still buttoning her sensible fawn woolen wrap over her nightgown, and with her wispy gray hair tucked up in a rather haphazard way beneath her crumpled white night bonnet, she came grumbling down the staircase to the echoing black-and-white-tiled hall, where the fire had gone out and the only light came from the single circular window above the main door.

Seeing the duke and Deborah waiting there, she continued to grumble as she crossed the floor toward them. "What is the meaning of this?" she demanded, not knowing to whom she was speaking because the duke had merely informed the maid who'd answered the door that he wished to speak to the headmistress.

The duke was a little testy. "The meaning of this, madam, is that we've come to take one of your young ladies to stay temporarily with her mother."

"Take one of my . . . ? Sir, this is most irregular! I cannot be expected to accommodate such whims, not when I have a proper establishment to run."

"Madam, I care not whether it is irregular, and I am certainly not in the habit of acting upon whims. This is a matter of importance, and I suggest that you read this letter." The duke handed the headmistress the letter of authority written by Lady Ann, who had signed the letter in her married name, Lady Ann Arrowsmith.

By now Miss Algernon had had a moment or two to observe the visitors more closely and realized that the gentleman at least was a person of some consequence. Clearing her throat awkwardly, she accepted the letter and broke open the seal. She read in silence until she reached the point where Lady Ann named the two persons who were to be entrusted with her daughter. "The Duke of Gretton?" she gasped, her face going pale as she raised her eyes to his.

"Madam." He inclined his head, but as she resumed her reading, he glanced at Deborah and smiled. The smile spoke volumes. This is one time, it said, when my rank receives the respect it is due.

Deborah found herself smiling as well and had to lower her gaze in case the headmistress should observe her silent amusement.

Miss Algernon folded the letter and cleared her throat once more. "You, er, must forgive me, Your Grace, for I had no idea who you were. Of course you may take Christabel to her mother." Turning, she beckoned to the waiting maid. "Inform Mrs. Johnson

160

that she is to prepare Christabel Arrowsmith to leave immediately.''

Deborah was a little anxious. ''Please do not alarm Christabel, Miss Algernon, for her mother is quite well.''

The headmistress nodded at the maid.

''Madam.'' Bowing, she hurried away up the staircase.

Miss Algernon gave Deborah and the duke a rather self-conscious smile. ''Would you, er, care for some refreshment? Some tea, perhaps?''

Before Deborah could reply, the duke accepted the offer. ''That would be welcome, Miss Algernon.''

''Please come this way, for there is a fire in my parlor.'' The headmistress conducted them across the hallway toward a pedimented door, beyond which lay her own private room. It was very comfortable and warm, and when the curtains were flung back the early morning sunlight streamed in to brighten the gold-and-white furniture and striped gray silk on the walls.

When she had shown them inside, the headmistress evidently decided against risking further faux pas and so left them alone. Deborah went to the window and gazed out toward the grounds and the cedar drive. There were daffodils on the lawns, and just beneath the window the flowerbed was bright with crocuses.

The duke came to stand at her shoulder. ''I trust you have recovered from your nightmare now, Deborah?''

She turned swiftly toward him, for it was the second time he'd used her first name.

He smiled a little, reading her thoughts. ''Do you mind if I call you Deborah?''

''You may do so if you wish, sir.''

"I wish, but only provided you pay me a similar compliment, and call me Rowan."

"I will do that." Her cheeks felt warm, and her hand moved to touch the locket.

His glance followed the action and he turned away, deliberately changing the subject. "I trust Miss Algernon will not be long in bringing Christabel," he murmured.

They said nothing more, for at that moment the door opened and a maid came in with a tray of tea. It was about half an hour after that that the headmistress returned with Lady Ann's rather bewildered daughter.

Christabel was the image of her portrait and the image, too, of her mother at the same age. She was on the verge of beautiful womanhood, with a flawless olive skin and the largest dark brown eyes imaginable, and she wore a simple white muslin dress with a wide pink velvet sash. Her dark hair was worn in ringlets, and her manner was timid and unsure as she looked at the two strangers into whose custody she was to be given.

Deborah understood her uncertainty and went quickly over to reassure her. Taking the girl's cold hands, she smiled. "Please don't be afraid, for we are your mother's friends. She wants to see you for a while, and—"

"But she is in Bath for the cure at the moment, surely she cannot want me to be there?"

"She will explain everything to you herself, and awaits you now. You will be with her soon." Deborah prayed the girl would not press for too detailed an explanation, for it was difficult to know exactly what to say.

To her relief Christabel did not ask any more questions, and a short while afterward, when the horses were sufficiently rested, the carriage departed from the school, soon coming up to a smart pace for the thirteen hilly miles back to Bath.

Chapter 17

At one o'clock that same day, Deborah and Lady Ann waited with Rowan in the conservatory at his house, for at any moment Sabrina was expected to return from Claverton Down. She would have to return soon, for she had to keep her two o'clock appointment with Madame Beauclerc, the appointment at which she believed she was to be faced with the reproaches and accusations of Richard Wexford's sister.

They weren't waiting to bring everything to a conclusion now, for although Sir James would bring Sabrina home, he would be permitted to leave again without anything being said to him. It was Sabrina herself they wished to speak to now, so that she could be told the truth and a final plan could be hatched to turn the tables upon the man whose machinations were the cause of so much pain and unhappiness.

The sun stood high in the heavens now, and it was such a beautiful spring day that the doors of the conservatory stood open to the garden. Daffodils, jonquils, crocuses, and hyacinths bloomed colorfully beside the brick path, and there was blossom opening on the shrubs and fruit trees growing against the wall of the mews lane. The two canaries sang in their gilded cage by the open doorway, their exuberance matched by the song of the wild birds outside, and to the earthy scent of the exotic plants in the conservatory was added the aroma of the Turkish coffee in the elegant silver pot on the table where the two women sat waiting.

Deborah wore her pink-and-white dimity gown, and her dark hair was piled on her head. The gown had a scooped neckline filled with frothy lace, and there was more lace at the cuffs. A gray cashmere shawl rested over her arms, and apart from some simple gold earrings, her only other jewelry was the locket. She tried to appear relaxed as she sipped the coffee from a dainty gold porcelain cup, but in truth she was filled with nervous anticipation.

In the seat next to her, Lady Ann was far more at ease, as if she had suddenly found a vast new store of courage. Her turquoise fustian gown was very bright in the sunlight streaming through the glass all around, and her dark eyes were alight, for now that Christabel was safe, she was determined to do all she could to see Sir James Uppingham punished. She was a new woman, no longer pale and ill at ease, but buoyant and heartened at the prospect of soon being free of Sir James.

Rowan stood in the doorway of the conservatory, his back toward them both as he gazed at the garden. His hair was almost silver in the sunlight and his full-sleeved shirt very white, for he had left his wine red coat tossed idly over the back of one of the wrought iron chairs. He had been there for several minutes, and no one had spoken, but then he straightened and turned.

"I think it best if Uppingham is invited to dine here tonight," he said. "I fancy he will be surprised at the fellow guests he finds waiting for him."

Deborah smiled. "He can be guaranteed a severe dose of indigestion," she murmured.

His blue eyes met hers. "I sincerely hope so," he replied.

Just then there was a knock at the front door of the house. They all heard it quite clearly because the door into the entrance hall from the conservatory had not been closed. Without another word Rowan left the two women, who strained to hear if it was Sabrina and Sir James.

They heard the butler speak to Rowan. "It is a running footman from North Parade, Your Grace. He has brought a note."

Deborah sat back, lowering her eyes.

There was a moment's silence in the hall as Rowan read the note, then they heard his reply. "Tell her yes, I will come, hopefully within the hour," he said.

Deborah stared at the coffeepot on the table, for she was sharply reminded that the odds against her were formidable. How could any woman hope to compete against a rival like Kate Hatherley? The wisest thing was to stifle the feelings that had been so cruelly aroused since arriving here in Bath. But that was far easier said than done.

Kate's footman left again, and the butler began to close the door behind him, but then saw a carriage approaching along the crescent. "Your Grace, Lady Sabrina is returning!" he cried.

Deborah and Lady Ann listened as the carriage drew up outside, and Sabrina and Sir James entered the house.

Rowan's voice was all that was calm and natural. "I trust you enjoyed the display?"

Sabrina's reply was short. "Yes. Thank you." The

only way in which she could have been more brief was to have merely inclined her head without speaking.

Deborah and Lady Ann exchanged glances. Hadn't the morning gone well?

Sir James cleared his throat. "I, er, think the ceremonials went on a little too long," he explained.

"I fear that is often the case," Rowan replied lightly. "James, it occurs to me that it might be agreeable if you were to dine with us tonight."

"Thank you, Rowan. I will be delighted to join you."

Sabrina remained silent.

Sir James cleared his throat again, for her uncommunicative manner was very marked. "I, er, will see you tonight then," he said to her.

"Yes." It was plainly all she could do to be even remotely civil to him, and Deborah reflected that Rowan had been very wise indeed not to say anything to her before she'd set off for Claverton Down, for it was plain she could not have disguised her feelings.

Rowan saw Sir James to the door, and when it had closed he spoke to his sister. "I must speak with you, Sabrina."

"I . . . I have no time now, Rowan. I am expected at Madame Beauclerc's at two, and—"

"And you also expect to meet Mrs. Marchant there?" he interrupted.

There was a stunned silence.

He spoke again. "Sweeting, your secret is known to me. I am fully aware of your love for Richard Wexford, of your intended elopement with him, and of your hitherto concealed reluctance to proceed with the Uppingham match."

The two women in the conservatory heard Sabrina's dismayed response.

"No!"

"Yes, Sabrina. Don't look so alarmed, for I am not angry with you, disappointed maybe, but not angry. Why didn't you tell me?"

"I . . . I don't know what you're talking about," Sabrina replied, her voice trembling with misgiving.

"Sabrina, there is no point in denying it, for I have been told all about it. Besides, it may interest you to know that Wexford didn't steal Lady Ann's necklace, nor was he intimately involved with her. It was all a plot against him, and the hand behind the plot was Uppingham's."

Sabrina was so shaken that she couldn't reply.

Rowan spoke again. "If you wish to see Richard Wexford's honor restored, I think you should come with me to the conservatory, where there are two ladies to whom you should speak."

Deborah gazed toward the entrance as footsteps approached, and then at last she saw Sabrina. Her face was very pale, and her lilac eyes wide and nervous as she allowed her brother to usher her into the conservatory. But her steps faltered as she saw Deborah and Lady Ann.

"Rowan, what is this?"

"You must hear them out, Sabrina," he replied.

Lady Ann rose to her feet. "Lady Sabrina, I am here because I wish you to know that Mr. Wexford did not steal my necklace, nor was he anything more than an acquaintance to me. Sir James made me act against my will because I, like you, have a secret to conceal. I have a daughter about whose existence I have been shabbily reticent, and in order to keep the world from knowing about her, I allowed myself to be black-mailed by Sir James. He found out about you and Mr. Wexford and was prepared to do whatever he felt necessary in order to keep you. I am very sorry indeed for what I've done, Lady Sabrina, but now I wish to reverse all the damage if I can. Mr. Wexford is innocent, and if we all four unite to prove it, then Sir James cannot win.''

Sabrina stared at her. "It . . . it was all a lie?" she whispered.

Lady Ann nodded. "I gave Sir James the necklace, and he hid it in Mr. Wexford's carriage. The rest you know.''

Sabrina's gaze swung to Deborah. "Where is he? I must go to him . . .''

"I don't know where he is, Lady Sabrina,'' Deborah replied quietly.

There was pain in the other's lovely lilac eyes. "But you must know.''

"I wish I did. He wrote to me and sent me the pocket watch to keep it safe, but he did not tell me where he would go because I don't think he knew himself.''

Tears welled down Sabrina's cheeks, and with a choked sob she hid her face in her white-gloved hands. "Oh, Richard, Richard . . .'' she whispered brokenly.

Rowan put his arm around her shoulder and led her gently to one of the chairs, where he made her sit down. "If I'd known how you felt, I would never have gone ahead with the Uppingham match. You had only to have shown a little reluctance, and nothing on earth would have permitted me to force it upon you. It doesn't matter how much Father wanted the marriage, for your happiness is what counts.''

Trying to overcome her tears, she put a shaking hand over his as it rested on her shoulder. "I felt so guilty for having been seeing Richard in secret, and then I believed he had really stolen the necklace, and that he had been betraying me with Lady Ann. The thought of being found out and exposed to ridicule and scandal was too much for me, and I thought that there was sufficient affection between Sir James and me for the match to work. But the more I am with him, the more I dislike him, and today I could hardly bear to be in his company. Even if this hadn't happened, I was going to tell you that I wish to be released from the contract." She drew a long, shaking breath. "And now that I know what he has done, I despise him with all my heart. Oh, poor Richard . . ." Fresh tears filled her eyes, and she was so overcome that she couldn't say anything more.

Rowan bent to draw her little hand to his lips, and then he enclosed it comfortingly in his. "As Lady Ann said, if we four unite, then Uppingham can be made to pay the necessary price. It is in order to embark upon this that I asked him to dine here tonight. It isn't going to be at all the agreeable social occasion he expects, for he is going to discover that the excellent hand he has held until now has been trumped in no uncertain fashion. I believe I know how to not only make Uppingham accept the blame himself for the theft of the necklace, and thus clear Richard Wexford's name, but also how to ensure that no scandal ensues for either you or Lady Ann. Believe me, my first impulse was to call him out for his crimes, but duels never remain secret, and the tale would get out. My second impulse was to see that he answered properly to the law, but too much would be broadcast over the land if he came to court. He would have the opportunity to invent what he pleased about you and Lady Ann. So, having considered all the probabilities, I think it best if Uppingham is, er, obliged to write a confession about the necklace, and if he is then allowed time to leave the country.''

Sabrina turned to look quickly up at him. ''Allow him to escape scot-free?''

''Hardly scot-free. He will have failed in his ultimate objective, winning you, and he'll be forced to kick his heels in some faraway place. I have Jamaica in mind, for a ship leaves Bristol on the morning tide. And he will know that you are with Richard Wexford.''

''If only we can find him.'' Sabrina got up slowly from her chair and faced Deborah. ''Is there nowhere you can think of where Richard may have gone?''

''Nowhere at all. He could have come to me at St. Mary Magna, but he didn't, and it's obvious he didn't go home to Wexford Park, for if he had he would have been arrested. He could be anywhere.''

Sabrina bit her lip, trying to blink back the tears that were still so very close to the surface. ''I feel so guilty. I should have known he wouldn't have done those things, but I was weak and selfish and chose to believe it rather than stand up for him as I should have done. I only hope that he will forgive me.''

Deborah smiled a little. ''Lady Sabrina, he loves you, so of course he will forgive you.''

''I will never forgive myself,'' Sabrina replied softly.

Rowan took her hand again. ''You and he will have a happy future together with my blessing, I promise you that, but first we must dispose of Uppingham. I want us all four to be ready for him when he arrives, for it is important that he knows we are unified against him. I know that Lady Ann and Mrs. Marchant are strong enough to face him, but are you strong enough, sweeting?''

Sabrina smiled at him. "Rowan, now that I know Richard is innocent, I am strong enough for anything. I will do whatever is required to see that he is exonerated, and after that I will do whatever I can to make up for failing him. I love him, and even if I admit it only belatedly, I mean to be true to him and to myself from now on.''

Lady Ann looked away. "You are fortunate indeed to have the chance to put matters right, Lady Sabrina. I now wish with all my heart that I had done the right things all those years ago, but for me it is too late.''

Deborah looked at her. "Not entirely, Lady Ann, for you could take Christabel to your father. Maybe he despised your late husband, but how could he possibly despise a girl as lovely and gentle as your daughter? Whatever his feelings about the past, Christabel is still his own flesh and blood, his granddaughter, and I cannot believe that he will reject her, or you.''

Rowan nodded. "I agree with Mrs. Marchant, Lady Ann.''

"I will think about it," she replied but in a tone that conveyed grave doubts. "I would like to shake off all the secrecy, but I am still afraid of causing my father's health to fail. Such past transgressions on my part will seem very heinous to him and perhaps far too shocking and great for him to accept.''

Deborah got up. "I think perhaps you and I should go home, Lady Ann, for you must wish to be with Christabel now that she is here in Bath.''

"Yes, I do indeed," Lady Ann replied, getting up as well.

Rowan put on his coat. "I will escort you both to your door," he said, and then remembered something. "Sabrina, I know that I was supposed to take you to Milsom Street, but I'm afraid my plans have changed and I am expected elsewhere now."

Deborah looked away, for he was expected at Kate's.

Sabrina gave a sudden smile. "Rowan, you don't honestly imagine I am still going to my dressmaker, do you? I couldn't stand still enough. I don't know whether I'm nervous or excited about tonight. I only know that soon everything is going to be all right again, and that is all that matters."

Chapter 18

There was a full moon that evening as Rowan arrived in person to escort Deborah and Lady Ann back along the Crescent for the fateful dinner. Lady Ann was already waiting in the drawing room with her daughter and Mrs. McNeil, who were to remain behind, and Deborah had yet to come down, but she appeared at the top of the staircase as Sanders admitted him.

Her dark hair was twisted up into an elaborate Grecian knot, with soft curls framing her face, and she wore the silver gray silk gown, long white gloves, and amethysts she'd worn to the theater. She hesitated before going down toward him, for suddenly she remembered that night at the theater, and the moment when she'd been leaving and she'd seen him kissing Kate Hatherley by the stage door. He had been with his mistress that afternoon . . . She drew herself up sharply, for what business was it of hers where he had been? She had no right to be jealous. But she was. Very jealous.

He saw her and came to the foot of the stairs to meet her as she began to descend. He wore a plum velvet coat, white silk breeches, and there was a ruby in his cravat. "You look very lovely," he said, smiling.

"Thank you." Her heart was turning over with wild

emotion simply at looking into his eyes. Please don't let him see how he affected her.

"You wore that gown to the theater, did you not?"

"How observant you are, sir," she replied.

"Sir? My name is Rowan," he corrected, taking her hand and drawing it to his lips.

She suppressed a shiver of pleasure. "How observant you are, Rowan," she repeated.

"I must speak privately with you, Deborah," he said, glancing briefly at Sanders, who waited nearby to assist the ladies with their cloaks when they departed.

But there was no opportunity to say anything more, for at that moment they both realized that Mrs. McNeil had emerged from the drawing room. If she had heard them address each other by their first names, she gave no sign.

She smiled at Rowan. "Good evening, Your Grace," she said, her oyster taffeta gown rustling as she came toward him.

"Good evening, Mrs. McNeil." He bowed.

"May I offer you some refreshment? I know you are only a few steps away from your house, but it seems churlish not to extend the hospitality of this house."

"There is no time, Mrs. McNeil, but I thank you for your thoughtfulness. If Uppingham should decide to arrive early, it wouldn't do for him to see me escorting Mrs. Marchant and Lady Ann along the pavement."

"No, it wouldn't do at all," she murmured, her glance encompassing Deborah for a moment. "I will tell Lady Ann that it is time to leave," she said then, turning back into the drawing room.

Deborah was very conscious of the older woman's

fleeting glance, for it had been very eloquent and her cheeks felt a little hot as she went to Sanders for him to place her cloak around her shoulders.

Mrs. McNeil returned with Lady Ann and Christabel, who still wore the white muslin gown she'd had on since leaving the school early that morning. Lady Ann had changed for dinner, and now wore sea green satin and opals. The light of determination and revenge was still bright in her eyes, but it softened lovingly as she turned to smile at Christabel.

"Mrs. McNeil will look after you, my dear, and I will return as soon as possible."

"Yes, Mama."

Lady Ann kissed her daughter's cheek, and then went toward Sanders, who waited with her cloak.

A moment later they all three stepped out into the silvery night, where the full moon shone clearly down from a starlit sky. It was very cold after the warmth of the day, and there would probably be a frost before morning.

Mrs. McNeil stood by the window with Christabel, the curtain held sufficiently aside for them both to watch as as the shadowy figures hastened along the pavement toward the house at the end. As the door of the other house closed behind them, Mrs. McNeil lowered the curtain and turned back into the drawing room.

Christabel looked at her. "The duke is very handsome, is he not, Mrs. McNeil?"

"Too handsome by far," was the murmured reply.

Sabrina was waiting in the entrance hall as her brother returned with their two accomplices. She was very fresh and lovely in cream lace and pearls, and although she was nervous about the evening ahead, she was no longer as pale and strained as she had been.

When the two ladies had once again been assisted with their cloaks, Sabrina began to conduct them into the drawing room, but Rowan called Deborah back.

"With your leave, Deborah, I really wish to speak privately with you."

"Privately?" She went back to him. "What is it?"

"Not here. Please come into the conservatory."

Puzzled, she followed him. The moonlight streamed unhindered through the glass panes, and the greenery all around seemed more luxuriant than it had in the sunshine. The night air seemed to release the scent of the flowers, so that there was an almost heady fragrance all around as he led her to the table and chairs. The canaries' cage had been placed there as well to keep them safe from the night chill of the glass, and the little yellow birds hopped from perch to perch as they were disturbed by Rowan's voice.

"Forgive me for seeking to be alone with you like this, Deborah, but there are things I wish to say to you," he said, turning to face her.

She paused by the cage, resting a gloved hand upon the gilded ironwork. "Say whatever you will," she replied, wondering what was on his mind. He seemed a little uneasy, as if he found it difficult to broach the matter.

His glance flickered to her amethyst necklace. "You aren't wearing your locket," he said suddenly.

"My locket? No, I prefer this necklace with this particular gown."

"The locket is obviously very precious to you." His eyes were intensely blue, even in the moonlight.

"Yes, it is." She had to look away, for suddenly she

was in her dream again, and the sea was sweeping Jonathan away before her horrified, guilty eyes.

"I understand that you have been living in seclusion for some time now. I took the liberty of quizzing Sabrina. She knew a little from your brother."

"Jonathan and I were very happy together, Rowan, and when he died I thought I would die, too. Seclusion is perhaps not the right word for my existence, isolation describes it more accurately. I chose to live alone at St. Mary Magna, and it was only the injustice being done to my brother that lured me away." She searched his face in the moonlight. "Why do you wish to know?"

He came a little closer, and the silver light shone on the diamond pin in his neckcloth. "Because I have noticed that when you wear the locket, you frequently touch it, as if clinging to memories. I know that it is no business of mine, and I apologize if my interest offends in any way, but widowhood is a strange and indeterminate state. For some it is fleeting and soon forgotten, and for others it is more painful but does come to an end, but for a few it is a state of endless grief for that which is lost forever and can never be replaced. Are you one of those last few, Deborah?"

She was surprised at such a direct and personal question.

He smiled a little ruefully and ran his fingers through his steely hair. "Forgive me, my interest transgresses," he said.

"It doesn't transgress, Rowan; it just caught me off guard. If you had asked me that question before I left St. Mary Magna, I would have said that yes, I do belong to that unhappy few, but now that I have gone out in society again, I no longer feel that I do." Because of you, because you've turned my whole world upside down, and because you've stolen my foolish heart with your smiles and kisses. Oh, yes, your kisses . . :

He came to her, taking her gloved hand and raising it to his lips. "Deborah, I—" He broke off in exasperation as the butler hurried in. "Yes, what is it?" he snapped.

"Sir James's carriage is at the door, Your Grace!"

"Very well, I will be there in a moment. Don't show him into the drawing room just yet."

"Very well, Your Grace." The butler hastened away again.

Rowan returned his attention quickly to Deborah. "There isn't time for me to say anything more now, but maybe tomorrow? A drive to Beechen Cliff, perhaps?"

"A drive? But—"

"I *must* speak alone with you, and for long enough to say all I wish."

For a moment she almost declined. She thought of Kate, with whom he had been that very afternoon, but then she nodded. "A drive to Beechen Cliff would be very agreeable," she said, dismayed at her weakness. Where was her pride? Had he demolished her standards as well as her defenses?

He smiled. "It is settled then," he murmured.

They heard the front door knocker, and he took her hand again, but instead of kissing it as he had before, he drew her closer, bending his head suddenly to brush his lips over hers. Then he was gone, walking swiftly out of the conservatory to greet Sir James as he was admitted.

She remained where she was, her eyes closed as she savored the echo of his kiss.

In the hall Rowan was all graciousness and cordiality. "Good evening, James, I trust you are in hearty appetite?"

"I will be, provided you are able to reassure me that Sabrina is well."

"She is much better this evening; indeed she is better than she has been in well over a week."

"Indeed?"

Deborah hurried to the entrance of the conservatory and peeped out. The two men stood in the middle of the hall. Sir James wore a charcoal silk coat, and his Apollo curls shone in the light of the chandelier. His manner was unguarded, for he had no inkling of the trap yawning before him.

Rowan was still all charm. "If you will come into the drawing room, Sabrina is waiting . . ." he stated, ushering Sir James toward the door.

As they went inside Deborah hurried across the hall behind them, and she was in time to see Sir James's stunned reaction as he saw Lady Ann with Sabrina by the fireplace.

His face went pale, and a wary look entered his eyes as he turned to look quickly at Rowan. "I, er, did not realize there would be another guest," he began, but then his pale eyes moved to Deborah as she appeared in the doorway. "What's this?" he demanded, every instinct warning him that something was very wrong.

Rowan gave him a cool smile. "This is your undoing, Uppingham. Your malevolent activities are known to me, and to Sabrina, and as far as you are concerned this is the end of the road."

Sir James's tongue passed swiftly over his suddenly dry lips, but then he dissembled, turning back to Sabrina and smiling. "Sabrina, I'm afraid I don't understand. What am I supposed to have done? If I offended you at the display this morning, then I beg your forgiveness, but I really have no idea in what way I have upset you.''

Sabrina's lovely face was cold. "This has nothing to do with this morning. I am no longer a gullible fool, sir, for I know what you did to Richard. He is the one I love, and he is the one I mean to marry, not you. I despise you, sirrah, for you are surely the lowest insect I ever knew, and I am ashamed that I was ever taken in by you. You aren't worthy of the name of gentleman, and I wish I had never heard your name, Sir James. After tonight you may be sure that I will never have anything more to do with you.''

The chill, condemning words were uttered in a steady tone that was devoid of all feeling, except loathing, and Sir James found himself gazing into lilac eyes that offered him no hope.

For a long moment he was too shaken to respond, but then once again he found his wits. Another smile played upon his full lips, and he gave a rather incredulous half laugh. "Look, I really don't know what all this is about. What am I supposed to have done to Wexford? I take it that it is Wexford to whom we are referring?''

Lady Ann raised her chin. "I have told them everything, Sir James, and if you still think to threaten me through my daughter, let me warn you that she is safely beyond your reach now. Let me also warn you that she is legitimate, and that you will be very wrong indeed to accuse me of having had a child out of wedlock. I had excellent reasons for keeping her a secret, but now I mean to acknowledge her, so your threats are powerless.''

There was an ugly twist on Sir James's lips as he turned to face Rowan. "What do you want of me? I presume you've lured me here tonight for some purpose?"

"Oh, yes," Rowan replied softly, "I have a purpose, of that you may be sure. You see, you may have been able to manipulate others until now, but I fear that it is now your turn to dance to order. You are going to admit to stealing the diamond necklace yourself, and to concocting the tale of theft simply to blacken Richard Wexford's name."

"I don't intend to admit to anything," Sir James replied.

"Uppingham, nothing would delight me more than to be given the excuse to snuff you out, but other matters have to be considered in this. I am not requesting you to write a letter of confession, I am telling you." With a cool smile Rowan indicated a writing desk in a corner of the room where fresh vellum, ink, and pens had been set out in readiness, together with a candle to melt the wax for the seal.

Sir James's tongue passed over his lips again. "And if I refuse?"

"I believe you know my reputation with a pistol, and if you don't, I promise you that you will soon learn firsthand whether I am the shot I'm famed to be. Of course I have the advantage of already knowing what a poor shot you are, for I've seen your appalling performance on the grouse moor."

Sir James swallowed. "Why bother to extract a written confession from me? Does it mean that you intend to put an end to me anyway?"

"I have already said that there are other considerations that prevent me from that happy course."

"Well, you would say that, wouldn't you? But with my written admission of guilt, it would be very convenient for me to meet with an accident."

"So it would, but unfortunately I do not wish to fall foul of the law myself. However, let me remind you that I am a very determined man, and I always get exactly what I want. In this instance I want you alive, but safely far away from England."

"Why?" Sir James searched his face shrewdly, and then glanced toward Sabrina and Lady Ann, a new light entering his pale eyes. "You're afraid of the courts!" he declared, his tone dangerously close to a taunt.

Rowan calmly drew a chased silver pistol from his coat and leveled it at Sir James's temple. "Far be it from me to insist upon compliance, Uppingham, but I fear that that is the way of it," he said dryly, pushing the barrel against Sir James's perspiring skin. "Now then, let us come to some sort of understanding, mm? You sit down like a fine fellow and write the required letter, and in return I will allow you sufficient time to leave the country and avoid arrest. Oh, I almost forgot, I have two very large henchmen waiting to escort you. Bristol is your destination, Uppingham, and the vessel that leaves on the morning tide for Jamaica. A few years in the Indies would be the very thing for you, don't you think? You look so pale and sickly at the moment that I fancy a little sun might be a sovereign remedy."

"If you think I will oblige you by agreeing, you must be mad!" Sir James cried then.

The pistol jabbed warningly. "Don't be difficult, Uppingham, for this is no jest. The last thing I intend is for you to have your say in court, and that is the only reason you are being offered exile as an alternative. But I have property in Jamaica, and my spies will be everywhere on the island, so that I will know of your every move and of your every unguarded word. Let anything slip to the detriment of any lady in this room, and you will have me to answer to. If you fancy the notion of having to glance constantly over your shoulder in case I am there, then by all means refuse to do as I ask. The choice is really yours, but I feel that the sensible decision would be to accommodate me in this. Of course, I may run out of patience in a moment, and my finger may twitch . . . Accidents do happen, as you've already pointed out.''

Sir James was visibly trembling now, and beads of perspiration stood out on his brow, which was ashen with fear. Gone was his bravado and swagger, and instead he had become a craven coward. He nodded. ''Very well, I will do as you ask.''

''Good. The writing desk awaits.'' With the pistol Rowan gestured toward the corner.

The room was silent as Sir James sat down and picked up a pen. Bright color and anger still marked Sabrina's cheeks as she watched him, but Lady Ann's face was calm. She now had nothing but contempt for him and wished with all her heart that she had defied him from the beginning.

Rowan glanced at Deborah, who still remained in the doorway. Their eyes met, and he smiled at her. She returned the smile and knew that she loved him.

At last Sir James sanded the vellum, shook the sheet, and then held it out to Rowan. ''Will that suffice?'' he asked.

Rowan read the letter, and then nodded. ''Well, since you shoulder the blame for stealing Lady Ann's necklace and hiding it in Richard Wexford's carriage in order to make it appear that he was the guilty party, then yes, it will suffice. But don't take any of my warnings lightly, Uppingham, for I meant everything, and if I feel obliged to break the law by putting an end to you, I will do so.''

''There won't be any need, for I will abide by your wishes in this.''

''See that you do.'' Rowan tossed the sheet of vellum down again. ''Seal it.''

Sir James folded the letter, and then held the sealing wax to the candle. Allowing the molten wax to drip on the the folded sheet, he then pressed his signet ring into it, leaving a perfect imprint of his cartwheel device.

Rowan went to the table and picked up the handbell. The butler hurried in immediately.

''Your Grace?''

''All is ready. You may take our, er, unwelcome guest out to his escort.''

''Your Grace.'' The butler bowed, and then turned expectantly to Sir James. ''Sir?''

Slowly Sir James rose from the writing desk. ''Am I to be permitted sufficient time to settle my affairs and pack?''

''If you can do so within an hour, then yes, otherwise I fear not, for you are going to be on that vessel when she leaves on the morning tide. And don't imagine that you will escape your guards, for they have been very well paid to keep a close watch on you. They will receive more if they deliver you safely on board, and so they have a vested interest in seeing to it that they carry out my instructions.''

Sir James's pale eyes moved toward Sabrina. "I did it because I love you, Sabrina," he said.

She didn't respond, except to turn her back toward him.

Without another word Sir James left the drawing room, not even glancing at Deborah as he passed. The butler gave him his cloak, and then opened the door. Two men stood there, and as Sir James emerged, they seized his arms and propelled him toward his carriage.

As the whip cracked and the vehicle drew away, Sabrina suddenly put her hands to her face and burst into tears. Lady Ann turned swiftly to comfort her.

"It's over now, my dear."

"It w-won't be over until we f-find Richard," Sabrina sobbed, clinging to the older woman.

"We'll find him," Lady Ann replied reassuringly.

A lump began to rise in Deborah's throat as well. Richard's name had been cleared, but he did not know it. He still believed himself to be pursued by the law for something he hadn't done, and he believed he had lost forever the woman he loved so much. If only they knew where he was, so that they could tell him all was well.

Rowan came to her, taking both her hands. "We'll find him, I promise you," he said softly.

"I pray you are right."

"I am right, Deborah, for I will not rest until this has been resolved to the satisfaction of all concerned." He smiled into her tear-filled eyes. "We are all going to emerge from this with our due measure of happiness."

Chapter 19

Rowan escorted Deborah and Lady Ann back to their quarters not long after that and left them to regale Mrs. McNeil and Christabel with the details of what had happened, but as they reached the door, he detained Deborah for a moment to remind her that they were to take a drive together the following day.

"I trust tonight's excitement hasn't wiped other matters from your memory?"

"Other matters?"

"We agreed to take a drive tomorrow."

"I have not forgotten," she replied.

"I will call at two o'clock."

She smiled. "I look forward to then."

"As I do," he said. "Good night, Deborah."

"Good night, Rowan."

Afraid that he would be able to see the love in her eyes, she turned and hurried into the house, and after a moment he retraced his steps along the pavement.

She entered the drawing room to find Lady Ann already relating the satisfactory sequence of events concerning the defeat and exile of Sir James Uppingham.

Mrs. McNeil was exultant. "So, in the immortal words of the great bard, 'all's well that ends well'!" she declared triumphantly.

Lady Ann nodded, and then reached over to take her daughter's hand. "Christabel, my dear, I came to a long overdue decision tonight, but even if it is overdue, it is still final. I mean to take you to meet your grandfather."

Christabel's eyes widened. "The earl? But—"

"No buts, not any more. I should never have been so weak and timid that I kept you a secret all these years. We will leave Bath for Hertfordshire as soon as possible."

Mrs. McNeil rose from her chair and went to ring for Sanders. "Tonight is too important not to be suitably toasted," she said. "I think that a bottle of my niece's champagne is called for, don't you?"

Deborah expressed as much delight as the others at this suggestion, but inside she knew that for her at least it wasn't yet time for champagne. Oh, she had achieved what she had set out to do, and Richard's honor had been restored, but there was now the new dimension of her love for Rowan. She was afraid to hope too much, for although he had kissed her tonight and invited her to drive with him tomorrow, she might still be reading far too much into what might after all be merely his way. She had surrendered her heart far too quickly, and she knew it herself, even without Mrs. McNeil's warning. Had she conveyed entirely the wrong impression when she had permitted things to take the course they had in order to fool Sir James's coachman? Did Rowan now think that she was ripe for the plucking, and regard her as a pleasurable diversion, to be enjoyed for a while before he discarded her in order to resume his passionate liaison with Kate Hatherley?

Some time later, as the ormulu clock on the mantelpiece struck midnight, Lady Ann got up from her chair. "I suddenly feel very tired indeed. I fear that champagne after all that excitement and strain has made me horribly drowsy."

Mrs. McNeil nodded. "I feel exactly the same, even though I wasn't actually at the scene. I fear that tomorrow is going to be inordinately dull for us all."

Lady Ann went to her and kissed her cheek. "Good night, Morag. I'm so glad that I've been able to wipe my slate clean and become truly restored to your favor."

"I'm glad, too."

A running footman was sent to engage two sedan chairs to convey Lady Ann and her daughter back to Great Pulteney Street, and within half an hour Mrs. McNeil and Deborah were alone together.

The older woman surveyed the younger shrewdly. "Your joy was somewhat reserved, my dear," she said.

"I won't feel it's truly over until we've found Richard."

"Oh, maybe that's part of it, but I fancy the Duke of Gretton is also greatly on your mind."

"I'd rather not talk about it, Mrs. McNeil."

"I'll warrant you would, for uncomfortable facts seldom sit easily upon our shoulders. Deborah, my dear, you aren't a green girl; you're a mature woman who knows the ways of the world. Rowan Sinclair is one of the most eligible and desirable men in the land, and he is also in love with his mistress. Common sense alone must tell you where that places you in his scheme of things. I do not deny that he appears to be showing an interest in you, but you must be very wary as to why he is doing so. If you are content to provide a few hours of pleasure for him, then by all means be foolish enough to do just that, but if you value yourself, as I think you do, then you will draw back from danger.''

''You do not tell me anything I do not know already,'' Deborah replied heavily.

''Then perhaps I need only say that I do understand how you feel, my dear. I may be past my prime now, but I had my moments in my youth. I know the all-consuming power of love and desire, and I know that you are in the grip of that power. Rowan Sinclair is the sort of man who would make a virgin saint throw caution to the winds, and you are neither a virgin nor a saint, but a woman who has known the joys of complete love, and who misses those joys. You are more vulnerable than you realize, my dear, and I am so afraid that you are going to suffer great hurt at the hands of the Duke of Gretton.''

''I know the hazards, Mrs. McNeil.''

''Then take my advice and act accordingly.''

''I am going for a drive with him tomorrow afternoon. I think I will know then what his purpose is.''

Mrs. McNeil studied her. ''Yes, my dear, you probably will, but what if his purpose is base?'' she asked quietly.

Deborah didn't reply.

After a moment Mrs. McNeil came to drop a kiss on her forehead. ''Just take care, my dear, that's all I ask. I don't want to see you hurt. Now then, I think we should both retire to our beds, don't you?''

''I'll come up in a while, Mrs. McNeil. I just want to sit here a little longer.''

''Very well. Good night, Deborah.''

''Good night.''

When the doors had closed behind the older woman, Deborah got up from her chair and went to extinguish all the candles, leaving the room lit only by firelight. She was about to resume her seat when she heard a carriage drive slowly along the Crescent from the direction of the Circus. It came to a halt somewhere nearby, and then there was silence. She didn't hear the opening or closing of the carriage doors or any voices. Her curiosity aroused, she went to the window and peeped outside.

The carriage was drawn up by the railings opposite. It was clearly visible in the light from a street lamp, and she saw that it was a dark green landau drawn by two cream horses. The hoods were raised, and there was no crest or coat-of-arms on its panels so that it was impossible to guess to whom it belonged.

Deborah drew the curtain back a little more, wondering why it had just halted there like that. Then, as she looked, a woman's face appeared at the tiny window. The face stared directly at her for a moment, pale and indistinct in the shadows, but then the door of the landau opened, and the woman alighted. She wore a white satin cloak with a hood, and as she stepped down, the hood fell back for a moment. Deborah could suddenly see her face and hair quite clearly. It was Kate Hatherley.

The actress crossed the road toward the house and quite obviously intended to come there. Instinct told Deborah that she was the only one upon whom Kate would call at this hour, and that whatever Rowan's mistress had to say to her was best said in complete privacy, and so she went to open the door herself just as Kate reached the steps.

The actress's brown eyes flickered, and a faint smile

touched her lips. "Can it possibly be that you expected me, Mrs. Marchant?"

"No, I didn't expect you, I merely happened to see you alight."

"Just as I saw you looking out." Kate stepped past her into the hall, bringing with her the faintest hint of roses from the scent she wore.

Deborah closed the door quietly and glanced up the staircase for a moment, but all was quiet, and Sanders had not realized that anyone had called. "If you will come this way," she said to Kate and conducted her into the drawing room, closing the door behind them so that they would not be overheard unless they raised their voices.

"Please be seated," she said to Kate, gesturing to any of the chairs.

"I do not think that this is the sort of call that requires much coziness, Mrs. Marchant," Kate replied, turning to face her, her tumbling chestnut curls shining in the firelight.

"Then what sort of call is it?" Deborah inquired guardedly.

"I think you already know. I've come here because of the Duke of Gretton."

Deborah said nothing.

Kate's dark eyes were cool. "I don't intend to behave like a lady, Mrs. Marchant, and if you think that I will stand idly by and allow you free rein to set your cap at Rowan Sinclair, you are sadly mistaken. I saw in a moment how you felt about him, and I also saw that you believed he was interested in you, or at least you hoped he was."

"When I came to your house my sole concern was clearing my brother's name, and if you imagined you saw anything else in my reason for being there, then you are the one who is sadly mistaken.'' Deborah held the woman's eyes. ''You know why I followed him there, and you assisted in persuading him to go with me. For that I will always be grateful to you, and I would prefer it if our acquaintance could remain on that amiable note.''

''Our acquaintance can never be amiable, Mrs. Marchant, not when we both want the same man.'' Kate's eyes flashed. ''Oh, don't play the innocent with me, for I have been with him since then, and I *know* what you're up to. Well, the gloves are off, my dear, and from now on I will do all in my power to turn him against you. He's mine, and he's going to remain mine.'' The dark eyes swept Deborah scornfully from head to toe. ''Do you honestly imagine that you have what it takes to triumph over me? I have made love-making an art, and when I decide that I want to keep a man's interest, then I do not fail. I have forgotten more than you have ever known, and I know how to gratify his every fantasy and whim. From now on he will know even more pleasure in my arms, and you may be sure that if he amuses himself with you, he will soon find you dull and return to me. Forget that at your peril.'' Kate's eyes glittered in the candlelight. ''He is spending tonight with me, and that is something else you should not forget.''

With that the actress turned and left the room. She went out into the night, leaving the front door open behind her, and Deborah remained in the drawing room as the carriage drew away. Then she went slowly out to the door, inhaling deeply of the frosty air before closing the door and leaning back against it.

Was he really going to spend tonight with his mistress? Please let it not be so; let it be a falsehood on Kate's part, designed to deter a rival. Let Kate's actions tonight be a lesser equivalent of the lies Sir James Uppingham had devised to rid himself of Richard Wexford.

Deborah closed her eyes, for she knew it was a vain hope.

Chapter 20

She slept very badly that night. Every time she closed her eyes, she saw Rowan lying with his mistress between silken sheets, and she could even imagine them speaking of her, and smiling at her naivete. At last it became too much of a torment, and she got up from the bed.

Her long coal black hair fell in untidy profusion about the shoulders of her white nightgown, and the glowing light of the fire was reflected in her gray eyes as she went to sit by the fire. She was bewildered by the strength and speed of her feelings for Rowan, for nothing like this had ever happened to her before, not even when she'd first known Jonathan. It was as if she were being swept along by forces beyond her will, and that all control was being denied her. Common sense bade her to protect herself, but there was no room for common sense when she remembered how she had felt when he'd kissed her on the steps by Lady Ann's house. A raw, heady desire had seized her then; her whole body had ached with a need that only he had aroused. She had wanted to surrender all to him, and she still wanted to.

The fire shifted in the hearth, and the clock struck half past five. At this time yesterday she had been changing to drive to Chippenham with him, and Mrs. McNeil had been seated in this very chair. *Take care, my dear, for when this is over* . . . When this was over, what then? What would life be for Deborah Marchant?

With a sigh, she got up restlessly from the chair. Perhaps a glass of hot milk would be the thing to help her relax enough to sleep. Putting on her wrap, she lit a candle from the fire, and then left the room.

The house was dark and silent as she made her way down the staircase and then along the passage past the archway to the door leading to the kitchen in the basement. The last time she had come this way, Rowan had been waiting for her.

As she entered the kitchen, for the most fleeting of moments it was as if he was there again. She thought she saw him by the fire, smiling as he turned toward her, but there were only shadows. Her hand trembled a little as she put the candlestick down upon the table, and the light quivered over the room for a moment before becoming steady once more.

The milk pail was kept on a marble slab in the pantry, and she took a small copper saucepan from a hook on the wall, but as she did so, there was a stealthy tapping at the window pane.

With a startled cry she dropped the pan, and her heart began to pound as she whirled anxiously about to stare at the window. A shadow moved, and the tapping came again, but a little more urgently. Then she heard a muffled voice.

"Deborah? It's me, Richard. Let me in."

Her eyes widened with disbelief. "Richard?" she repeated incredulously.

He pressed his face closer to the glass, and at last

she saw that it was indeed her brother. A glad cry escaped her lips as she ran to the door. Her fingers were shaking so much that she could barely turn the key in the lock or drag the bolts back, but at last she succeeded, and in a moment she was in his arms.

"Oh, Richard!" she cried, hugging him tightly, half laughing, and half crying at the same time.

He felt cold as he held her, and the iciness of the predawn night swept bitterly into the warm kitchen, bringing with it the smell of frozen earth and trapped chimney smoke. Then he released her and turned to push the door to before facing her. He had her gray eyes and almost black hair, but he looked strained and anxious. He wore a rather crumpled ankle-length brown greatcoat with a sable collar, and he looked tired as he tossed his tall hat and gloves down upon the table next to the candle, making the solitary flame leap and dance.

Deborah gazed at him through tears of joy. "I can't believe you're here," she whispered. "I—"

"And *I* can't believe *you* are here either," he interrupted coolly.

Her smile faltered. "Richard, I—"

"Do my feelings mean nothing to you, Deborah? I trusted you to do as I asked, but instead you decide to play the loyal sister and come here to right all the wrongs. No doubt your motives are admirable, but I do not appreciate them at all. I went to St. Mary Magna to see you because I felt so wretched and alone that I could not bear it any longer. I wanted to be with the one person in the world whom I felt I could trust beyond all shadow of doubt. I arrived there only to be told by Briggs that you'd come here the moment you received my letter. I don't for a moment imagine that your purpose was simply to spend some socially agreeable time with Jenny and Henry, or that you've come here for the cure. Deborah, if you've caused Sabrina any embarrassment or distress, I will never forgive you.''

Tears still shimmered on her lashes, but they were tears of hurt, not of happiness. ''I couldn't let things remain as they were, Richard, for I love you too much for that.''

''But I *wanted* you to leave things as they were!'' he cried. ''The last thing on God's earth I've ever wanted is for Sabrina to have to face any hint of gossip. If she and I had managed to elope and marry, then she would have had the protection of my name, and we would have weathered the storm together, but—''

Deborah couldn't bear it and had to interrupt. ''Richard, Sabrina knows that you are innocent, and so does her brother. Lady Ann was being blackmailed by Sir James, who tonight wrote a confession that clears your name entirely. Sir James is at this moment en route for Jamaica, and we only need your presence to make the triumph complete. Sabrina loves you, and the duke will give you both his blessing to wed if that is what you wish.'' Her voice shook, and the words came out in a rush.

Now it was his turn to stare. His lips parted and then closed again, and suddenly he leaned both hands on the table and stood with his head bowed. ''I . . . I cannot believe it,'' he whispered.

She went to him, putting a tentative hand on his shoulder. ''But it is true, Richard, and it came about because I decided not to abide by your wishes, and so I make no apology. I would do it again.''

He turned toward her then, crushing her into his

arms and resting his cheek against her hair. "Forgive me, Deborah, forgive me for finding fault, and for speaking so harshly."

She slipped her arms around his waist. "You were not to know that it had all come to so satisfying a conclusion."

He drew back, taking her face in his hands. "And Sabrina really does still love me?"

"Yes. Sit down, and I'll tell you everything that has happened since I arrived here. Well, nearly everything," she added, deciding that it would be best to be completely discreet about her own affairs.

He listened intently as she related the story of how Sir James Uppingham had met his downfall, and when she finished, he smiled at her. "What a veritable thorn you've been, Deborah Marchant. I will be eternally grateful."

She looked away, for Rowan had once used those very words to her. "You must rest for a while now, and then we can both go to see Sabrina in the morning," she said, going to pick up the saucepan and replace it on its hook.

He watched her. "What's wrong, Sis?" he asked after a moment.

"Wrong? Nothing."

"I know you better than that. You said earlier that you would tell me nearly everything. What is it that you've omitted to tell?"

"There isn't anything," she replied.

"When it comes to pretending on my behalf, you are apparently very adept, but when it comes to yourself, you are very unconvincing indeed. Deborah, you've done so very much for me, that it is a little selfish of you not to allow me the chance to offer help in return.''

She looked away. ''There is nothing you can say or do that will make any difference, Richard, I . . .'' She couldn't finish and turned away again so that he couldn't see how close to tears she was.

He got up and came to her, taking her by the shoulders and making her look at him again. ''Tell me,'' he ordered firmly, holding her gaze.

She hesitated, and then drew a long breath. ''Richard, we are a brother and sister in love with another sister and brother,'' she said quietly.

He stared at her. ''You and Rowan Sinclair?''

''I love him, but everyone knows he loves Kate Hatherley.''

''Oh, Deborah,'' he breathed, kissing her forehead and then pulling her comfortingly into his arms.

Mrs. McNeil was overjoyed to be awoken early the next morning with the news that Richard had returned. Still in her night bonnet and gown she hurried from her bed and down to the breakfast room, where he was enjoying a very hearty breakfast indeed.

He rose swiftly from his chair to hug her, for he had always been as fond of her as she was of him, and when she had finished weeping with delight that he had turned up at such a very advantageous moment, she made him sit down again and tell her all that had been happening to him.

Deborah sat with a cup of coffee and a slice of untouched toast. She wore a blue-and-white gingham morning gown, and her dark hair was piled into a knot on top of her head, with a blue satin ribbon fluttering loose to the nape of her neck. There was a frost outside, but the sun was already melting it, and the clear skies promised another beautiful day. She smiled as she watched Mrs. McNeil's undisguised delight, as she listened again to Richard's story of the inns and stables he'd slept in before he'd gone to St. Mary Magna. She wished she could join in the general joy and delight, but just as had happened the evening before with the champagne celebration, she was too apprehensive on her own account. Mrs. McNeil was right, for how could she possibly prevail over a rival as dazzling and seemingly invincible as England's most beautiful and fascinating actress?

Shortly after breakfast she and Richard hurried along the pavement toward the house at the end, for he hadn't been able to contain himself a moment longer, but simply had to be reunited with Sabrina.

His greatcoat had been attended to by the laundry maid, and there was a lightness in his step. He was transformed, not only outwardly, but inside as well. A great weight had been lifted from his shoulders, and now all that remained to make his happiness complete was to be with his beloved Sabrina again.

At his side Deborah was almost fearful of being admitted to the house. What if Rowan wasn't there? What if he had indeed spent the night with his mistress?

Richard knocked at the door, and the startled butler hastened to open it. "Mr. Wexford? Oh, Mr. Wexford, do come in!" he cried on seeing who stood there.

They entered the quiet hall, and the butler hurried up the staircase to tell Sabrina who had called. They heard her undisguised cry of joy, and a moment later she appeared at the top of the staircase. She wore a lace-trimmed nightgown, and there were no slippers on her feet as she ran down to fling herself in Richard's arms.

They were locked in an embrace, their lips together in a long, sweet kiss, and both their faces were flushed with love as she drew back to turn to the butler.

"Please tell the duke that he must come down immediately," she said.

Any gladness Deborah felt on learning that he hadn't spent the night away was speedily replaced by intense dismay when the butler replied.

"His Grace went to North Parade late last night, my lady, and he has not returned."

Chapter 21

Two o'clock had long since past, and the afternoon light was beginning to fade as Deborah stood waiting in vain by the drawing-room window, gazing across at the daffodils in Crescent Fields. She wore a lavender silk pelisse over a white muslin gown, and there were lavender plumes curling down from the crown of her leghorn bonnet. She was dressed for the carriage drive to Beechen Cliff that had not taken place, and as the minutes continued to tick relentlessly by, she knew that Kate had won the brief battle for the Duke of Gretton—if battle it had ever been, for when it came to choosing between his mistress and Deborah Marchant, there had apparently been no real contest at all.

Of course it was vaguely possible that he had been detained somewhere, for he had taken Sir James's confession to the authorities, and the truth about who had stolen Lady Ann's necklace was now known all over Bath. When Richard had driven with Mrs. McNeil to call upon Lady Ann, he had been recognized, and a great stir had been caused. No one as yet knew about Christabel, for it was Lady Ann's intention to say nothing until she had taken her daughter to the family seat in Hertfordshire the next day, and, of course, no one knew about Richard and Sabrina, for gossip was to be avoided at all costs.

Deborah stared across Crescent Fields. Yes, it was possible that Rowan had been unavoidably detained, but it was far more likely that he had forgotten all about the promised drive, or indeed that he had chosen to forget it. Kate had sworn to satisfy his every need, and that was precisely what she would have done, thus making absolutely certain that her upstart challenger had paled into complete insignificance.

Turning from the window, Deborah went to hold her hands out to the fire. She had been the end in fools to allow a man like Rowan to enter her heart, and she should have accepted the truth with some semblance of dignity when she learned where he had spent the night, but instead she had allowed herself to hope. She had dressed with care for the drive, telling herself that he would come, but he had not, and here she was, still waiting. He had yet to even return to his house, and was no doubt at this moment languishing in Kate's arms, without even a passing thought for the foolish one he'd so swiftly and easily beguiled.

The door opened behind her, and she turned to see Mrs. McNeil coming in. The older woman wore a fawn taffeta gown that rustled busily as she crossed the room to put an understanding hand on Deborah's arm. "This won't do, you know, my dear," she said gently. "Why don't you go upstairs and change into your afternoon gown? No one need ever know that you waited for him."

"I will know."

"It was bound to come to this."

Deborah swallowed. "Well, you did warn me, and I chose not to take any notice."

"My dear, I doubt if the day will ever come when we women can be relied upon to do the sensible thing, not when it comes to matters of love. The Duke of Gretton is the sort of man to turn even the stoniest heart, and you, my poor Deborah, do not have a stony heart. Far from it."

"I will know better in future, you may be sure of that," Deborah murmured, gazing into the fire.

"Well, that's as may be, but for the moment we must think how to show him that you don't give a fig. You must proceed as if there had never been any arrangement to go to Beechen Cliff and—"

"I have decided to leave Bath first thing in the morning," Deborah interrupted quietly.

"Oh, my dear . . ."

"I don't want to stay here, not when I am bound to see him. Besides, there is no need for me to stay here, and quite suddenly the thought of St. Mary Magna is very enticing indeed. I came here only to see if I could clear Richard's name, and now that that has been done, there is no need for me to stay."

"If that is what you really wish, my dear, then there is nothing more I can say, except that I think it is the wrong decision. For your pride's sake, it would be better if you remained here and at least gave yourself the satisfaction of cocking a snook at him, even if the snook was a pretense."

"I'd rather not see him again, if possible. I just want to go home and forget this aspect of my stay here. You do understand, don't you?"

"Yes, my dear, I understand perfectly."

"I will leave at first light in the morning."

"So early?"

"It's best," Deborah said, and then had to choke

205

back a sob that rose suddenly in her throat. Gathering her skirts, she hurried from the room.

Mrs. McNeil felt close to tears herself, but they were tears of anger. "Plague take you Rowan Sinclair, and may it consign you and your wretched mistress to perdition itself!" she muttered at the empty room.

Dawn was just breaking as Deborah's traveling carriage drew up at the door. The horses' breath stood out in clouds in the frosty air, and the lamps cast pools of pale light in the shadows as Sanders opened the door of the house and two footmen carried the first trunk out to be loaded. The Crescent was quiet, and there were no lights at any of the windows along the elegant sweep of houses. Bath was serene in the first early grayness of the new morning, and there was a luminosity about the sky that promised another beautiful spring day. But as Deborah prepared to leave, there was still no sign of Rowan.

Richard and Mrs. McNeil waited in the drawing room. He wore a blue paisley dressing gown belonging to Henry Masterson, and his hair was tousled from sleep. Mrs. McNeil's hair was plaited and without powder, and she had on her peach velvet wrap. They neither of them spoke, for what was there to say that had not already been said. They had both tried to persuade Deborah to stay, but nothing would move her.

They exchanged glances as at last they heard her descending the staircase with Amy, who was once again armed with the very necessary lavender pomander. Then the maid hurried on out to the waiting carriage, and Deborah came into the drawing room to say her farewells. There were shadows under her gray eyes, and her face was pale, but she gave a brave smile. She wore the fur-trimmed gold velvet cloak she had had on for the outward journey from St. Mary Magna, and her hands were plunged into her muff, for it would be several hours yet before the sun was up and the air became less cold.

Richard met her eyes. "Please don't leave like this, Deborah, for there is no need."

"There is every need, Richard."

"He may not be with Kate Hatherley. Dammit, we don't know *where* he is!"

"He's with her," Deborah replied quietly, taking her hands from the muff and then going to embrace Mrs. McNeil. "Thank you for everything, Mrs. McNeil."

"It was nothing, my dear," the older woman replied, returning the hug.

"You were a sterling friend," Deborah answered. "Indeed, you were the only person here who was prepared to stand by the Wexford family, and that is something I will never forget." She turned to her brother. "Say good-bye to Sabrina for me, Richard."

He pulled her into his arms, crushing her close. "Of course I will," he muttered, and then drew back. "Do you wish to send a message to Rowan?"

"No."

"But—"

"There is nothing to say, Richard. I made a fool of myself and all I want now is to forget all about it."

"I feel so damned guilty."

"Guilty? Why?"

"Because if it wasn't for me, none of this would have happened."

Deborah smiled. "I've been taught an invaluable lesson, Richard, and I won't forget it in a hurry. Please don't feel guilty, for I don't blame you at all; in fact I'm delighted that you and Sabrina are together again, and that you will soon be able to acknowledge your love to the whole world.''

"After a suitable time," he murmured.

"But of course, for it wouldn't do at all for her to wear one man's ring one day, and another man's ring the next. Just think of the rattling teacups if that were to happen! The whole point of banishing Sir James to the Indies is to protect Sabrina from such gossip, so pray do not undo all the good work by hurrying things along.''

"We won't." He smiled, taking her face in his hands. "I wish you weren't going, for we've hardly had any time to talk."

"You and Sabrina must come to stay with me."

"I'd like that, and I'm certain she would, too."

"Come whenever you wish." Deborah hugged him again, and then turned quickly away.

They followed her to the door and stood watching as Sanders assisted her into the waiting carriage. Williams cracked the whip once, and the team strained forward. They watched until the vehicle had vanished toward the Circus, and then Mrs. McNeil looked toward the Sinclair residence.

"I trust I will be able to be civil to the duke when next we meet," she said.

"Mrs. McNeil, are you as convinced as Deborah that he is with Kate Hatherley?" Richard asked suddenly.

"Where else would he be?"

"I don't know, but I *do* know that he has never stayed away like this before without leaving word where he could be found. Sabrina is becoming a little concerned, for it isn't like him to leave her in the dark.''

"From all accounts, his mistress is keeping him fully occupied," Mrs McNeil replied dryly, recalling what Deborah had told her of Kate's visit.

"Maybe."

"Whatever he's doing, there is no excuse for letting your sister down as he has done. He asked her to drive with him yesterday afternoon, intimating that there were important private things he wished to say to her, and he simply did not come, nor did he even bother to send word. He has treated her in a very cavalier fashion, and I for one think less of him as a consequence. Maybe Deborah has been too trusting for her own good, and maybe she has brought this upon herself, but it does not alter the fact that as I understand it he gave her cause to hope. Last night I wished him in perdition, and this morning I still wish it. The cold light of a new day hasn't softened my attitude toward him. He has behaved shabbily, and that is the truth.''

Tossing another angry look toward the end house, Mrs. McNeil went inside. Richard remained on the doorstep for a moment longer. Was it the truth? Had Rowan simply behaved shabbily, or was there more to it? Maybe judgment should be reserved, for in his own experience the Duke of Gretton was not the sort of man to deliberately and callously cause pain and humiliation to someone like Deborah.

Bath slipped away as the sun rose above the eastern horizon, and Williams set the fresh horses along the hilly Chippenham road at a smart pace. Almost two hours after leaving Royal Crescent, the carriage passed the gates of Miss Algernon's academy, and Deborah glanced along the cedar drive toward the redbrick mansion. The journey so far had been accomplished over roads she had last traveled with Rowan, but from now on she could try to put him from her thoughts. It wouldn't be easy, for she had lost her heart and head completely, but she would forget him in the end. She had to.

The spring weather was clement, and the carriage made good time, reaching the Angel at Sherborne by nightfall. She cried herself to sleep in her room that night, and was awake before dawn again the next morning, unable to sleep properly both because she was so upset and because the inn was busy all night, with stages and mail coaches arriving and leaving throughout the hours of darkness.

After an early breakfast, of which she ate only a little, she continued on the road to St. Mary Magna, but no matter how much she tried to put Rowan from her mind, he was constantly there. If she glanced at a wayside cottage, she found herself remembering the drive to and from Chippenham. If she closed her eyes for a moment, she was in his arms in the darkness by Lady Ann's house, surrendering to the waves of heady desire that he had aroused. And if her gaze wandered to the new leaves beginning to unfurl in the hedgerows, her memory carried her back to that night in the conservatory, when he had suddenly kissed her. What possible reason could he have had for such a gesture, unless he had meant it? It had been that kiss above all else that had made her cling so foolishly to hope the following day. Every minute had seemed like an hour as she'd waited for his carriage to arrive at the door, and in the end she had had no option but to admit to herself that there was nothing to hope for.

Darkness had fallen by the time the carriage made its weary way along the valley of the River Chaldon, and then up the village street toward the church and the house, and as Williams reined in for the last time and Deborah alighted, she took a deep breath of the remembered air. There was a tang of salt from the sea and the fragrance of the jonquils among the daffodils in the gardens, together with the sweet scent of woodsmoke from the village chimneys.

She glanced around, at the oriel window facing down the street, at the tower of the church against the sky, at the river, and at the lighted windows of the cottages. She was home, and if it hadn't been that Richard's good name had been restored, she would have wished with all her heart that she'd never left.

Chapter 22

Over the following days Deborah embarked upon the daunting task of trying to forget the Duke of Gretton, but then, almost a week later, something happened to make that task totally impossible.

The weather had undergone another change, and instead of the balmy spring sunshine of recent weeks, there was wind and rain. In the cove the sea was stormy, with thundering waves and screaming gulls, and in the shelter of the St. Mary Magna valley the smoke was torn from the cottage chimneys as March roared out like a lion.

Deborah was seated in the winter parlor, with the volume of *Vathek* open on her lap. She wore a high-necked gray velvet gown with long sleeves and a wide gold-buckled belt around the waistline beneath her breasts. The locket was at her throat, her dark hair was twisted into a knot on top of her head, and there was a warm white shawl over her arms. The fire drew in the hearth as the wind moaned outside, and she gazed at the flames as they fluttered audibly around the logs. She had read two pages of the book, but that had been over an hour ago. Since then her thoughts had wandered, to Bath, and inevitably to Rowan.

She was still stricken to think she had allowed herself to hope so very much. It was now quite clear that he had never intended anything as far as she was concerned, and she had been guilty of immense naivete in interpreting such a great deal from so little. The embraces by Lady Ann's house had been simply the subterfuge he had described them as, and the kiss in the conservatory had been of no consequence whatsoever. She was mortified to think of how obvious she had been in her feelings toward him, so obvious that Mrs. McNeil had immediately perceived, and so had Kate Hatherley, the latter to such an extent that she had felt obliged to issue a timely and devastating warning.

The wind blustered around the eaves, and a shower of sparks fled up the chimney toward the lowering sky, where endless dark clouds raced inland from the sea. Beyond the village the windswept cliffs were bleak and exposed, and from time to time she could hear the distant roar of the foaming sea in the cove. She turned to glance out of the rain-washed oriel window toward the heights above the shore, and as she did so she heard a carriage driving at speed along the village street. It was coming toward the house.

Puzzled, she put her book aside and went to the window to look down into the street. The traveling carriage was a costly vehicle, its dark green panels spattered with mud from the open road. Its team of four chestnuts was tired and sweating as the coachman began to slow them in order to maneuver the vehicle before the door of the house. As the carriage wheeled about Deborah saw her brother Richard inside.

Richard? But why had he come to St. Mary Magna? She pressed her face to the glass and watched as he alighted. He paused for a moment, glancing toward the church where once he had been Jonathan's best man. He wore his brown greatcoat with the collar upturned, and his tall hat was tilted back on his dark hair. He looked a little strained, she thought, guessing immediately that something was very wrong.

As she looked he turned to extend a hand into the carriage, and a moment later Sabrina stepped down, her rose woolen skirts fluttering as the wind snatched at them. There was a jaunty straw bonnet on her head, but her manner was anything but jaunty as she clung anxiously to Richard's hand. Her face was very pale and wan, and she had obviously spent a great deal of time crying.

A pang of foreboding struck through Deborah as she gathered her skirts to hurry from the winter parlor and down through the house to greet them in the great hall, where Briggs had already realized a carriage had arrived and was going toward the door.

Reaching the foot of the grand staircase, Deborah halted, watching as the butler admitted her unexpected guests. The wind blustered damply into the house as Richard ushered Sabrina inside.

Briggs was pleased to see him again. "Why, Master Richard, what a pleasure this is . . ." he began, but his voice died away as Sabrina suddenly saw Deborah and hurried across the stone-flagged floor to seize her hand.

"Please tell me you've heard from Rowan! Please!" she implored.

"I . . . I haven't heard anything, Lady Sabrina."

Sabrina's lips trembled, and distraught tears welled from her eyes. She turned instinctively toward Richard, and he hurried to take her in his arms, enclosing her in a comforting embrace.

"It's all right, my darling, we'll find him," he murmured reassuringly.

Deborah looked anxiously from one to the other. "What has happened?" she asked.

Sabrina drew herself together. "Rowan hasn't been heard of since the night Richard returned to Bath. He hasn't sent word to anyone, and no one has any idea at all where he might be."

Deborah stared at them both. "But surely someone must know."

Sabrina shook her head. "It's so unlike him, Mrs. Marchant, for he is always so meticulous about letting me know where he will be, even to the extent of his visits to Mrs. Hatherley. He always felt that if something went wrong and I needed him urgently, then I should know where to send word. As you know, he left word with the butler that night that he would be visiting North Parade, but that is the last we have heard."

Richard met his sister's eyes. "It's becoming very worrying now, Deborah, for it is totally out of character for him to go away like this. We know that he spent a little time with Kate Hatherley, and that when he left her he said he was coming home to Royal Crescent. But he didn't arrive there, and both he and his curricle have simply disappeared. Sabrina and I have dispensed with any pretense about our relationship, for she has needed me with her these past days. I fear that the precautions to keep Uppingham's tongue from wagging have proved pointless, for the whole of Bath is now aware that we have long since ceased to be mere acquaintances. The teacups are rattling, as you may imagine, for there is a great deal for them to rattle about. There is not only the business with Uppingham, but also the sudden advent of Lady Ann's daughter, my close friendship with Sabrina, and now Rowan's disappearance. Bath hasn't been in such a state of scandalized turmoil in many a year.''

Sabrina dabbed her eyes with a lace-edged handkerchief. ''I don't care about the gossip. I thought it was to be dreaded, but now that I am so worried about Rowan, the gossip is of no significance at all. I would endure a great deal more notoriety than this if only my brother were safely home again.'' She looked tearfully at Deborah. ''Did he say anything to you which might give us a hint as to where he might have gone?''

''To me? Lady Sabrina, it is very unlikely that he would have said anything of consequence to me, for I was a mere acquaintance.''

Sabrina glanced briefly at Richard, and then returned her attention to Deborah. ''Richard told me how you felt about Rowan, Deborah. May I call you Deborah?''

''Yes, of course.'' Deborah felt awkward color flooding into her cheeks, and she gave Richard a reproachful look.

Sabrina swallowed. ''I know that you love my brother, Deborah, and I know that he felt sufficient regard for you to wish to go for a drive alone with you.''

''He did not keep that appointment, Lady Sabrina,'' Deborah pointed out quickly.

''But he meant to, I'm sure of it. I know that it is a faint hope that you might know something, but once I thought of you, nothing would do but that Richard brought me here immediately.''

''I wish I could help, truly I do, but he didn't say anything to me. I believe that the person who might know something is Kate Hatherley, for he spent that night with her, and—"

"He didn't spend the night with her," Sabrina interrupted. "He went to see her, but he didn't stay. We know this because Richard went to see her, and she said Rowan stayed only a while and the last she had seen of him was when he left her house in his curricle, having informed her that he was coming home to Royal Crescent. She has now left Bath herself, having suddenly decided to terminate her contract with the Theatre Royal and return to London."

"And he didn't say anything to *her* that might tell us . . . ?"

"No, nothing at all." Sabrina's voice became choked with fresh tears. "Where is he, Deborah? I'm so afraid for him now that all this time has gone by, and now I'm beginning to dread what might have befallen him. Something is very wrong, for he would not leave me in ignorance as to his whereabouts. Deborah, I'm so fearful that he might be dead."

Deborah closed her eyes, her fingers tightening convulsively on the handrail of the staircase. No, please, no. Rowan couldn't be dead.

They stayed for two days, but then Sabrina became restless and wanted to return to Bath in case there was news there. They wanted Deborah to accompany them, but she decided to stay in Dorset. Promising to send word to her the moment they learned anything, they set off in the continuing wind and rain, and Deborah was alone once more. But it was a different loneliness now, for it was tinged with apprehension that the news when it came would be very bad indeed. She didn't want to admit to her fearfulness, but it was there all the time, hovering on the edge of her consciousness, tormenting her when she slept, and gnawing at her courage when she was awake. The weather confined her to the house, and she spent hour after hour by the oriel window, watching the rivulets of rain trickle down the glass.

March gave way to April, the daffodils faded and were replaced by the brilliance and fragrance of wallflowers, and at last the storm clouds rolled away and the skies were clear and blue once more. The sun shone down over the countryside, and the leaves unfurled to the richest and freshest of greens. It was a day upon which to escape from enclosing walls and ride up on the clifftops, and when the sun was at its height, Deborah rode out of the stable yard and along the village street.

She wore her russet riding habit, and the white gauze scarf fluttered lightly from her beaver hat as she urged her mount up out of the Chaldon valley toward the cliffs. The smell of the sea was fresh and clean, and the gulls were very white against the heavens as they wheeled on the light breeze. It was very different now from the last time she had come up here, for then it had been as stormy a day as the one on which the *Thetis* had foundered. This was Dorset at its glorious best, so beautiful and timeless that it was hard to imagine the elements becoming violent and cruel enough to drive a frigate onto the rocks.

She reined in above the cove, gazing down at the clear blue water as it lapped so mildly against the shore. She had not thought a great deal about Jonathan in recent days, but she thought about him now. She had grieved for him for three long years, and during that time she had acknowledged over and over how much she loved and missed him. The grief was still there, but the edge had gone from it. Life moved on, and it was the present that mattered, not the past. Her love for Jonathan would always be there, but it now took second place to her love for Rowan.

She drew a long, trembling breath. Was fate about to cruelly consign her to fresh grief? Please don't let that happen. Please. It did not matter if he did not love her, or if it was Kate Hatherley who held him in her arms, just as long as he was safe and well.

Her horse shook its head suddenly, its ears pricked as something caught its attention in the valley behind. Deborah turned in the saddle, shading her eyes with her hand as she watched a light vehicle skimming along the tree-lined lane toward the village. It was drawn by two high-stepping grays, and as it slowed to negotiate a narrow stone bridge over the River Chaldon, she saw that it was a scarlet curricle.

Her heart seemed to miss a beat. Surely it couldn't be. . . ? The thought remained unfinished as she gathered the reins and urged her mount away from the cliffs toward the distant tower of St. Mary's church.

The curricle had already arrived at the house as she reined her sweating horse in on the gravel nearby. She stared for a long moment at the perfectly matched grays and the curricle's shining panels, then she dismounted and hurried into the house.

After the brilliance of the sunshine outside, it seemed so dark in the great hall that she couldn't distinguish anything, but then a shadow moved by the fireplace, and she turned swiftly toward it. It was Rowan.

He wore a sky blue coat and close-fitting cream cord breeches, and there was a jeweled pin in the folds of his lace-trimmed neckcloth. His tall hat and gloves lay upon a nearby table next to a bowl of wallflowers, and his silver hair shone in a shaft of light from a high window as he took a few steps toward her. He smiled. "I fear I am somewhat late for Beechen Cliff, Deborah."

Her eyes became accustomed to the gloom, and she saw with a shock that he was thinner than he had been before, and his face had lost its usual tan. "What happened to you?" she asked. "Everyone has been so worried . . ."

"I've already been back to Bath to see Sabrina, and so I know the furor my absence has caused. As to what happened to me, well, I fear that I met with an accident and lay unconscious for some time."

"Unconscious?" Her eyes widened with concern.

He smiled again. "I do believe you are anxious for me."

"We have all been anxious for you."

"Ah, yes. Well, I gather that you know I left Kate's with the intention of going home to Royal Crescent. I was doing precisely that when it occurred to me that if I drove to Bristol I could be absolutely certain that Uppingham was on that ship when it sailed. With a curricle Bristol is not far, and so I set off. I reached the port in time and saw the vessel set out with him safely on board. I began the drive back, but took the wrong road and found myself miles away from where I should have been. I saw a track which I thought would lead me back to the Bath road, but instead it took me out into the wilds somewhere, and then the curricle lost a wheel, overturned, and I was thrown into a gully. I was knocked unconscious and lay there for several days before a shepherd found me. I was still unconscious when he took me to his family, and they looked after me until I came around three days ago. I managed to get the curricle repaired, recompensed my hosts handsomely for their help, and then drove to Bath. I found that you had come back here, and I learned from Sabrina and Richard why you had done so.''

She turned away. ''What did they say?'' she asked, endeavoring to make her voice sound light.

''I think you already know the answer to that. Deborah, I did not spend that night with Kate, because I went to see her only in order to end my liaison with her.''

She turned quickly. ''To end it?''

He nodded. ''You surely do not imagine that I behaved as I did toward you out of idle caprice?''

She lowered her eyes a little guiltily.

''Deborah, I knew my affair with Kate had to be ended, and what is more she knew it too, because when I'd seen her earlier in the day I'd tried to bring it all to a close then, but it had proved inordinately difficult because I was so anxious not to hurt her.''

''So that was why she visited me,'' Deborah murmured, trying to sound calm when all the time her pulse was racing unbearably.

''I wanted to speak privately with you before Uppingham came, because I wanted to tell you then what was in my mind, but as you know there was no time, and so I decided to wait until the drive to Beechen Cliff instead. When Uppingham had been disposed of and I had seen you home, I went to see Kate again, but I was very late indeed because I spent so long talking with Sabrina before she retired. It was because I was late that out of pique, Kate chose to call upon you. When I called and she finally realized that I meant to end our liaison, she told me what she'd said so spitefully to you, and that made me sufficiently angry to close matters once and for all. Our parting wasn't amicable, for I was outraged that she could have said such things to you.'' He came a little closer. ''Deborah, I know from Sabrina and Richard that you love me, and by now you must surely know that that love is more than returned.''

She stared at him, a wild elation beginning to sing through her veins.

''Come to me, Deborah,'' he said softly, holding out his hand.

She took a hesitant step forward, and then suddenly his fingers closed over hers. An electrifying force seemed to fly through her, as if she had been slumbering but had been awakened.

His thumb caressed her palm. ''Sabrina is soon to become Lady Sabrina Wexford, much to the shocked amazement of Bath's stricter tabbies, and so I think it only fair that said tabbies should be positively thunderstruck by the further astonishing development that due to Richard Wexford's captivating sister, the Duke of Gretton has ceased to be one of England's most eligible noblemen. I want you to be my wife, Deborah Marchant.''

She gazed at him through a blur of unshed tears, and her body yielded against his as he slipped an arm around her waist and pulled her closer.

''Will you do me the inestimable honor of becoming my bride, Deborah?'' he asked softly. ''No other woman will do to be my duchess.''

''I can't believe you really want me, Rowan,'' she whispered.

"I want you very much, Mrs. Marchant, almost too much for me to remember that I am a gentleman. But when you become mine, it must be properly, and when I seal our love, it must be in a marriage bed. So what is your answer? Will you marry me?"

"More than willingly," she breathed, closing her eyes as he kissed her. Her lips parted beneath his, and she savored the sheer ecstasy of being in his arms. He was safe and well, and, unbelievably, he belonged to her.

How far away now that dreadful day when she had received Richard's letter and had first learned of Sabrina's secret love? And how even further away the long days of loneliness after losing Jonathan? Everything was different now, and a new life stretched before her—a life of happiness as the Duchess of Gretton.